W. Allen Whitworth

Exercises in Algebra

Anatiposi

W. Allen Whitworth

Exercises in Algebra

Reprint of the original, first published in 1875.

1st Edition 2023 | ISBN: 978-3-38282-806-6

Anatiposi Verlag is an imprint of Outlook Verlagsgesellschaft mbH.

Verlag (Publisher): Outlook Verlag GmbH, Zeilweg 44, 60439 Frankfurt, Deutschland
Vertretungsberechtigt (Authorized to represent): E. Roepke, Zeilweg 44, 60439 Frankfurt, Deutschland
Druck (Print): Books on Demand GmbH, In de Tarpen 42, 22848 Norderstedt, Deutschland

EXERCISES IN
ALGEBRA

TO SIMPLE EQUATIONS INCLUSIVE

WITH AN INTRODUCTORY LESSON ON
NEGATIVE NUMBERS

FOR THE USE OF

ELEMENTARY SCHOOLS

(GOVERNMENT STANDARDS IV. V. VI.)

BY

W. ALLEN WHITWORTH, M.A.

FELLOW OF ST JOHN'S COLLEGE, CAMBRIDGE, INCUMBENT OF
CHRIST CHURCH, LIVERPOOL,
Author of "Modern Analytical Geometry," "Choice and Chance," &c.

LONDON:
GEORGE PHILIP AND SON, 32 FLEET STREET.
LIVERPOOL: CAXTON BUILDINGS, SOUTH JOHN STREET.
AND 49 AND 51 SOUTH CASTLE STREET.
1875.

PREFACE.

THIS Manual is intended to accompany oral teaching from the black-board. A specimen of such teaching is given in the "Introductory Lesson."

My arrangement of the subject is distinguished by three points, two of which are, I believe, quite novel, while the third has a historical sanction, being, in fact, the temporary use, as a stepping-stone for the learner, of one of the stages by which the system of notation in present use was originally reached.

The three points are as follows :—

1. Instead of explaining − (*minus*) as a sign of operation, and afterwards showing that it may be a sign of affection as well, the reverse order is adopted.

2. Letters and symbols of quantity are not introduced until the first four rules and the use of brackets are thoroughly understood in their application to positive and negative numbers.

3. The notation of indices is not used until the pupil is familiar with such quantities as xx, xxx, &c.

The advantage is gained that the pupil has not to work in the dark with mysterious letters, the use of which he is not to understand until afterwards, but from the beginning he is really learning something and grasping some new ideas.

A good teacher will strive to excite in his pupil an enthusiasm for his subject. And even in the processes of elementary Algebra sources of pleasurable interest will be found, especially in the charms of symmetry and the excitement of rapid simplification. Therefore, in framing these exercises, I have had great regard to symmetry, and have largely provided for the gratification of that pleasure which we enjoy when we find that an expression, very complicated in appearance, is capable of being reduced to a very simple form.

I have not only put the most liberal construction on the Government requirement of "Algebra to Simple Equations inclusive," for Standard VI. of the New Code, but I have also added exercises on parts of the subject which, though they come logically within the defined limits, are not understood to be included in the requirements of the Education Department. Thus the student will find in the book every variety of exercise that he can require until he is ready to approach Quadratic Equations, which may come into a sequel.

The different points which the teacher will need to explain and illustrate as the student proceeds are indicated in small type, and a brief syllabus is given of the propositions which constitute the Theory of Fractions.

INTRODUCTORY LESSON.

———◆———

Teacher.—You all know how to count. Begin at seven.
Boys.—Seven, eight, nine, ten, eleven, twelve, thirteen.
Teacher.—How far can you go on ?
Boys.—As far as you like.
Teacher.—Then what is the highest number you know ?
Boys.—There is no highest number. If you mention a number as great as you like, we will name a greater one.
Teacher.—Quite right ! There is no highest number. If you could tell the number of the stars you could add one to that number and get a higher number. Now, can you count backwards from *seven.*
Boys.—Seven, six, five, four, three, two, one.
Teacher.—Go on ; what is the next number?
Boys.—Nothing.
Teacher.—Well, go on ; what next ?
Boys.—We cannot go any further.
Teacher.—Cannot you ? Then that is just what you are going to learn to do to-day.
1st Boy.—But there *cannot* be a number less than nothing.
3d Boy.—Nothing is the lowest number.
5th Boy.—To speak of less than nothing is nonsense.
Teacher.—Oh ! you were second in the class last week. How many places have you gained since?
5th Boy.—None.
Teacher.—Then you are in the same place still !
5th Boy.—No; I am lower.

Teacher. —Then you have gained *less than none.* Your progress has been *less than nothing.* Is not that so ?

Boys. —Yes, sir.

Teacher.—Then I am afraid *less than nothing* is not nonsense, is it ?

Boys.—No, sir.

Teacher.—Now, look at this picture of part of a thermometer tube. At the bottom of the tube there is a bulb filled with a fluid which rises or falls in the tube, according as the air around it is hotter or colder. If it is cold enough to freeze water the fluid just comes up to the figure O, and if it is hot enough to boil water it rises to the point marked 100, which is much too high to be shown in the picture. If the heat is anything between freezing and boiling, the fluid will come up to some number between O and 100 ; and the heat is described as so many *degrees,* according to the number reached by the top of the fluid. If the fluid comes up to A, what will the temperature be ?

Boys.—Five degrees.

Teacher.—And if it rises 10 degrees more, what will it be ?

Boys.—Fifteen degrees.

Teacher.—And then if it falls 12 degrees——

Boys.—The temperature will be three degrees.

Teacher.—Yes ; that is very near freezing-point. But suppose it falls five degrees more, what number will express the temperature then ?

Boys.—It will be less than nothing.

Teacher.—How much less.

3d Boy.—Two.

1st Boy.—The temperature will be two less than nothing.

Teacher.—You see we want names for all these numbers that

are less than nothing. Now they are named in a very simple way. Two-less-than-nothing is called *minus-two* ; three-less-than-nothing is called *minus-three*, and so on. Look at the picture again, and tell me what will be the temperature if the fluid only comes up to the point B.

Boys.—Minus-eight.

Teacher.—Quite right. Now, begin again, and count backwards from seven.

Boys.—Seven, six, five, four, three, two, one, nothing, minus-one, minus-two, minus-three, minus-four, . . .

Teacher.—Very good ; and now count forwards from minus-four.

Boys.—Minus-four, minus-three, minus-two, minus-one, no thing, one, two, three. . . .

Teacher.—Which is the greater number, minus-five or minus-eight ?

Answer.—Minus-five is the greater.

Teacher.—When we use the figures 1, 2, 3, &c., to represent the numbers one, two, three, &c., the same figures with a short line before them will represent minus-one, minus-two, minus-three, &c. Thus, − 25 is minus-twenty-five, and − 1000 is minus-a-thousand, Is that a very high number ?

Boys.—No ; a very low one.

Teacher.—And which is the lowest number ?

Boys.—There is no lowest number.

Teacher.—What was the lowest number you knew at the beginning of the lesson ?

Boys.—We thought *nothing* was the lowest.

1st Boy.—Now *nothing* seems to be a sort of middle number, for we can name as many numbers below it as above it.

Teacher.—The numbers greater than nothing are called positive, and the numbers less than nothing are called negative numbers. You can find the difference between any two numbers, whether they be positive or negative, either by counting on your fingers from the one to the other, or by looking at the place of each on the thermometer scale and counting the number of degrees marked between them. For example, you can find the difference between the two numbers *minus-eight* and *five* by counting the number of degrees between B and A on the scale. What *is* the difference between *minus-eight* and *five* ?

Teacher. —Then you have gained *less than none.* Your progress has been *less than nothing.* Is not that so ?

Boys. —Yes, sir.

Teacher.—Then I am afraid *less than nothing* is not nonsense, is it ?

Boys.—No, sir.

Teacher.—Now, look at this picture of part of a thermometer tube. At the bottom of the tube there is a bulb filled with a fluid which rises or falls in the tube, according as the air around it is hotter or colder. If it is cold enough to freeze water the fluid just comes up to the figure O, and if it is hot enough to boil water it rises to the point marked 100, which is much too high to be shown in the picture. If the heat is anything between freezing and boiling, the fluid will come up to some number between O and 100 ; and the heat is described as so many *degrees,* according to the number reached by the top of the fluid. If the fluid comes up to A, what will the temperature be ?

Boys.—Five degrees.

Teacher.—And if it rises 10 degrees more, what will it be ?

Boys.—Fifteen degrees.

Teacher.—And then if it falls 12 degrees——

Boys.—The temperature will be three degrees.

Teacher.—Yes ; that is very near freezing-point. But suppose it falls five degrees more, what number will express the temperature then ?

Boys.—It will be less than nothing.

Teacher.—How much less.

3d Boy.—Two.

1st Boy.—The temperat

Teacher.—You see we w

are less than nothing. Now they are named in a very simple way. Two-less-than-nothing is called *minus-two*; three-less-than-nothing is called *minus-three*, and so on. Look at the picture again, and tell me what will be the temperature if the fluid only comes up to the point B.

Boys.—Minus-eight.

Teacher.—Quite right. Now, begin again, and count backwards from seven.

Boys.—Seven, six, five, four, three, two, one, nothing, minus-one, minus-two, minus-three, minus-four, . . .

Teacher.—Very good ; and now count forwards from minus-four.

Boys.—Minus-four, minus-three, minus-two, minus-one, nothing, one, two, three. . . .

Teacher.—Which is the greater number, minus-five or minus-eight ?

Answer.—Minus-five is the greater.

Teacher.—When we use the figures 1, 2, 3, &c., to represent the numbers one, two, three, &c., the same figures with a short line before them will represent minus-one, minus-two, minus-three, &c. Thus, — 25 is minus-twenty-five, and — 1000 is minus-a-thousand, Is that a very high number ?

Boys.—No ; a very low one.

Teacher.—And which is the lowest number ?

Boys.—There is no lowest number.

Teacher.—What was the lowest number you knew at the ꞏ lesson ?

ꞏought *nothing* was the lowest.

ꞏ *nothing* seems to be a sort of middle num- ame as many numbers below it as above it. numbers greater than nothing are called posi- nbers less than nothing are called negative ꞏn find the difference between any two num- ꞏ be positive or negative, either by counting m the one to the other, or by looking at the ꞏ thermometer scale and counting the number between them. For example, you can find een the two numbers *minus-eight* and *five* by ꞏer of degrees between B and A on the scale. ꞏꞏe between *minus-eight* and *five* ?

Teacher. —Then you have gained *less than none.* Your progress has been *less than nothing.* Is not that so ?

Boys. —Yes, sir.

Teacher. —Then I am afraid *less than nothing* is not nonsense, is it ?

Boys. —No, sir.

Teacher. —Now, look at this picture of part of a thermometer tube. At the bottom of the tube there is a bulb filled with a fluid which rises or falls in the tube, according as the air around it is hotter or colder. If it is cold enough to freeze water the fluid just comes up to the figure O, and if it is hot enough to boil water it rises to the point marked 100, which is much too high to be shown in the picture. If the heat is anything between freezing and boiling, the fluid will come up to some number between O and 100; and the heat is described as so many *degrees,* according to the number reached by the top of the fluid. If the fluid comes up to A, what will the temperature be ?

Boys. —Five degrees.

Teacher. —And if it rises 10 degrees more, what will it be ?

Boys. —Fifteen degrees.

Teacher. —And then if it falls 12 degrees——

Boys. —The temperature will be three degrees.

Teacher. —Yes ; that is very near freezing-point. But suppose it falls five degrees more, what number will express the temperature then ?

Boys. —It will be less than nothing.

Teacher. —How much less.

3d Boy. —Two.

1st Boy. —The temperature will be two less than nothing.

Teacher. —You see we want names for all these numbers that are less than nothing. Now they are named in a very simple way. Two-less-than-nothing is called *minus-two*; three-less-than-nothing is called *minus-three*, and so on. Look at the picture again, and tell me what will be the temperature if the fluid only comes up to the point B.

Boys.—Minus-eight.

Teacher.—Quite right. Now, begin again, and count backwards from seven.

Boys.—Seven, six, five, four, three, two, one, nothing, minus-one, minus-two, minus-three, minus-four, . . .

Teacher.—Very good ; and now count forwards from minus-four.

Boys.—Minus-four, minus-three, minus-two, minus-one, nothing, one, two, three. . . .

Teacher.—Which is the greater number, minus-five or minus-eight ?

Answer.—Minus-five is the greater.

Teacher.—When we use the figures 1, 2, 3, &c., to represent the numbers one, two, three, &c., the same figures with a short line before them will represent minus-one, minus-two, minus-three, &c. Thus, − 25 is minus-twenty-five, and −1000 is minus-a-thousand, Is that a very high number ?

Boys.—No ; a very low one.

Teacher.—And which is the lowest number ?

Boys.—There is no lowest number.

Teacher.—What was the lowest number you knew at the beginning of the lesson ?

Boys.—We thought *nothing* was the lowest.

1st Boy.—Now *nothing* seems to be a sort of middle number, for we can name as many numbers below it as above it.

Teacher.—The numbers greater than nothing are called positive, and the numbers less than nothing are called negative numbers. You can find the difference between any two numbers, whether they be positive or negative, either by counting on your fingers from the one to the other, or by looking at the place of each on the thermometer scale and counting the number of degrees marked between them. For example, you can find the difference between the two numbers *minus-eight* and *five* by counting the number of degrees between B and A on the scale. What is the difference between *minus-eight* and *five*?

Boys.—Thirteen.

Teacher.—And what the difference between *three* and *minus-three?*

Boys.—We have to count from C to D on the scale—the difference is six.

Teacher.—What do you call the process of finding the difference between two numbers?

Boys.—Subtraction.

Teacher.—Well, we shall find another way of subtracting positive and negative numbers some day. But it will be a good exercise for you to-day to work as many examples as possible, by counting on your fingers or on the thermometer scale.

Find the difference between—

5 and − 5	5 and − 10	− 50 and − 70
8 ,, − 2	1 ,, − 12	100 ,, − 100
− 7 ,, − 4	− 1 ,, − 5	273 ,, − 127
2 ,, − 5	0 ,, − 8	
− 3 ,, − 2	− 7 ,, − 8	

EXERCISES IN ALGEBRA.

1. Add *one* to each of the following numbers :—

3	− 3	− 5	99	− 99
− 10	− 12	12	− 1	− 7
0	− 2	1	2	− 4

2. Add *two* to each of the numbers in Exercise 1.

This will be done by counting two from each given number, as in the Introductory Lesson.

3. Add *three* to each of the same numbers.

4. Add *five* to each of the same numbers.

5. Arrange the following numbers in order, beginning with the lowest and ending with the highest :—

20	− 19	− 21	− 10	9	11

6. Arrange in the same way the following numbers :—

0	10	− 100	1000	− 10000

7. Arrange in the same way the following numbers :—

0	− 10	100	− 1000	10000

Teacher.—Then you have gained *less than none.* Your progress has been *less than nothing.* Is not that so ?

Boys.—Yes, sir.

Teacher.—Then I am afraid *less than nothing* is not nonsense, is it ?

Boys.—No, sir.

Teacher.—Now, look at this picture of part of a thermometer tube. At the bottom of the tube there is a bulb filled with a fluid which rises or falls in the tube, according as the air around it is hotter or colder. If it is cold enough to freeze water the fluid just comes up to the figure O, and if it is hot enough to boil water it rises to the point marked 100, which is much too high to be shown in the picture. If the heat is anything between freezing and boiling, the fluid will come up to some number between O and 100 ; and the heat is described as so many *degrees,* according to the number reached by the top of the fluid. If the fluid comes up to A, what will the temperature be ?

Boys.—Five degrees.

Teacher.—And if it rises 10 degrees more, what will it be ?

Boys.—Fifteen degrees.

Teacher.—And then if it falls 12 degrees——

Boys.—The temperature will be three degrees.

Teacher.—Yes ; that is very near freezing-point. But suppose it falls five degrees more, what number will express the temperature then ?

Boys.—It will be less than nothing.

Teacher.—How much less.

3d Boy.—Two.

1st Boy.—The temperature will be two less than nothing.

Teacher.—You see we want names for all these numbers that

are less than nothing. Now they are named in a very simple way. Two-less-than-nothing is called *minus-two* ; three-less-than-nothing is called *minus-three,* and so on. Look at the picture again, and tell me what will be the temperature if the fluid only comes up to the point B.

Boys.—Minus-eight.

Teacher.—Quite right. Now, begin again, and count backwards from seven.

Boys.—Seven, six, five, four, three, two, one, nothing, minus-one, minus-two, minus-three, minus-four, . . .

Teacher.—Very good ; and now count forwards from minus-four.

Boys.—Minus-four, minus-three, minus-two, minus-one, no thing, one, two, three. . . .

Teacher.—Which is the greater number, minus-five or minus-eight ?

Answer.—Minus-five is the greater.

Teacher.—When we use the figures 1, 2, 3, &c., to represent the numbers one, two, three, &c., the same figures with a short line before them will represent minus-one, minus-two, minus-three, &c. Thus, — 25 is minus-twenty-five, and — 1000 is minus-a-thousand, Is that a very high number ?

Boys.—No ; a very low one.

Teacher.—And which is the lowest number ?

Boys.—There is no lowest number.

Teacher.—What was the lowest number you knew at the beginning of the lesson ?

Boys.—We thought *nothing* was the lowest.

1st Boy.—Now *nothing* seems to be a sort of middle number, for we can name as many numbers below it as above it.

Teacher.—The numbers greater than nothing are called positive, and the numbers less than nothing are called negative numbers. You can find the difference between any two numbers, whether they be positive or negative, either by counting on your fingers from the one to the other, or by looking at the place of each on the thermometer scale and counting the number of degrees marked between them. For example, you can find the difference between the two numbers *minus-eight* and *five* by counting the number of degrees between B and A on the scale. *What is the difference between minus-eight and five?*

14. Exercises in Addition :—

− 3	3	− 3	8	5	12
5	− 5	5	− 2	− 5	− 8
4	7	− 7	− 4	5	− 3
− 2	− 9	9	− 6	− 5	− 1
6	1	− 1	4	5	9

− 12	− 12	12	− 12	12	12
20	− 20	− 20	20	− 20	20
− 17	− 17	17	17	− 17	− 17
15	15	− 15	− 15	15	− 15
− 16	16	16	16	− 16	− 16
14	14	− 14	− 14	14	− 14

THE pupil has already learnt to find the absolute difference between any two numbers (positive or negative) by counting from the one to the other. This is the same thing as subtracting the less from the greater. The teacher will now explain how the subtraction of the greater from the less leaves a negative result. The pupil can then do the next exercises by counting to get the numerical difference, and then determining whether the result must be positive or negative.

15. Exercises in Subtraction :—

From	5	5	3	− 3	− 3	− 5
take	3	− 3	5	5	− 5	− 3

From	10	10	10	10	12	12
take	12	− 12	10	− 10	10	− 10

From	12	12	− 10	− 10	− 10	− 10
take / *12*	− 12	12	− 12	10	− 10	

From	− 12	− 12	− 12	− 12	0	0
take	10	− 10	12	− 12	10	− 12

From	17	− 13	− 11	15	− 21	16
take	− 16	15	− 13	12	21	− 16

THE teacher will now explain how the addition of a negative quantity is equivalent to the subtraction of a positive quantity, and the subtraction of a negative quantity equivalent to the addition of a positive quantity, illustrating it by the help of Exercises 17 and.18.

16. The following is a statement of my property:—I have £100 in the bank and £20 in my purse. I owe £30 to A, and £40 to B, and £10 to C. How much am I worth?

17. If a friend takes off my hands my account with A, how much is he taking from me. How much richer or poorer does it make me?

18. If in addition to the above accounts I owe £10 to D, how much does the addition of this account make me worth?

19. By remembering that the subtraction of any number is the same thing as the addition of the complementary number, work the following exercises in subtraction:—

From	0	0	− 3	− 3	3
take	1	− 1	3	− 3	− 3

From	1000	− 763	476	453	− 453
take	− 575	− 876	576	− 547	547

From	-760	-743	1	-1	-500
take	342	-233	500	500	500

IT is now seen that minus ($-$) may be used as a sign of subtraction, as it makes no difference whether we consider $5-3$ as meaning "*five* and *minus-three*," or as meaning "*five* and subtract *three*." In either case we have

$$5-3=2.$$

At the same time we may introduce plus ($+$) as a sign of addition.

20. Find the value of

$13-8+2$	$2-4-6$
$13+4-12$	$3+5-8$
$16+13-15+8$	$9-6+9-7$
$15-14+13-12$	$1-19-20+21$
$7-8+3+2-1$	$1-2+3-4+5$

21. Add

	-1		
	-1	-5	
	-1	-5	-7	-3
-4	-1	-5	-7	-3
-4	-1	-5	-7	-3
-4	-1	-5	-7	-3

IT is now time for the teacher to explain the multiplication of negative quantities.

> *three* times *four* is *twelve.*
> *three* times *minus-four* is *minus-twelve.*
> *minus-three* times *four* is *minus-twelve.*
> *minus-three* times *minus-four* is *twelve.*

Although it is difficult at first to see what *minus-three* times *minus-four* means, yet very little consideration leads to the conclusion that the result must be complementary to the result of *minus-three* times *four*.

22. Multiplication :—

-5×12	$8 \times (-12)$	$1 \times (-16)$
-12×5	$5 \times (-12)$	-1×3
$-12 \times (-5)$	$25 \times (-12)$	$3 \times (-1)$
$-5 \times (-12)$	-1×16	$-1 \times (-1)$

NOTE.—The bracket ( )' is inserted above only because it is awkward to let the two signs × − come together.

23. Find the continued product in the following exercises :—

$(-3) \times (-4) \times (-5)$ $3 \times (-4) \times (-5)$

$3 \times 4 \times (-5)$ $3 \times (-4) \times 5$

$(-1) \times (-1) \times (-1)$ $(-1) \times (-1) \times (-1) \times (-1)$

$(-1) \times (-1) \times (-1) \times (-1) \times (-1) \times (-1)$

IF division be understood to be the undoing of multiplication, the rule of signs in the division of negative quantities follows as a corollary from the rule in multiplication. Thus

> *twelve* divided by *four* gives *three,*
> *twelve* divided by *minus-four* gives *minus-three,*
> *minus-twelve* divided by *four* gives *minus-three,*
> *minus-twelve* divided by *minus-four* gives *three.*

Therefore, either in multiplication or division, two negative quantities produce a positive result, while a negative and a positive quantity produce a negative result.

24. Divide 6480 by each of the following divisors :—

$$3 \qquad -4 \qquad -5 \qquad 6 \qquad -8 \qquad -12$$

and divide − 6480 by each of the following divisors :—

$$10 \qquad -16 \qquad -18 \qquad -20 \qquad 27 \qquad 30$$

Also divide 3 by − 3 and divide − 3 by 3.

25. Find the value of
$$3 \times (-5) \quad + \quad (-5) \times (-8) \quad + \quad 8 \times (-3)$$
and of
$$3 \times (-5) \times (-8) \quad + \quad 2 \times (-8) \times (-2)$$
and of
$$(-18) \div 3 \quad + \quad 18 \div (-3) \quad + \quad (-18) \div (-3)$$
and of
$$9 \times (-8) \div 6 \quad + \quad 12 \times 25 \div (-10)$$

WHEN a number of quantities are included in a bracket, the bracket *tells us* that all the quantities inside it are to be treated as one quantity. *How* they are to be treated is shown by some sign outside the bracket. If we want to take away a bracket we must do what the bracket tells us. The teacher will illustrate this.

26. Find the value of

$3 \times (7 + 8)$	$4 \times (5 - 2)$	$6 \times (8 - 7)$
$5 \times (7 - 8)$	$(-3) \times (7 + 8)$	$(-4) \times (7 - 8)$
$(-1) \times (4 - 1)$	$(-2) \times (1 - 3 + 2)$	$3 \times (5 - 7 + 2)$

N.B.—When two quantities come together without any sign between them, the sign of multiplication must be understood to be between them, thus $5(3-7)$ means that 3 and -7 are to be multiplied by 5, and therefore
$$5(3 - 7) = 15 - 35 = -20.$$
$-4(2 + 3 - 8)$ means that 2 and 3 and -8 are to be multiplied by -4, and therefore
$$-4(2 + 3 - 8) = -8 - 12 + 32 = 12.$$
Similarly
$$5(3 - 7) + 8(4 - 1) + 2(1 - 3)$$
$$= 15 - 35 + 32 - 8 + 2 - 6 = 0.$$
And
$$3(4 - 6) - 4(2 + 3 - 8) - 5(1 - 5)$$
$$= 12 - 18 - 8 - 12 + 32 - 5 + 25 = 26.$$

27. Find the value of

$$3(5-7) \qquad 5(3+2-5) \qquad 7(1+2+3)$$
$$3(5-7)+2(3-6)+7(8-5)$$
$$5(4+3-5)+6(3-2+7)+8(5-7)$$
$$3(2+3)-5(3+4)+4(2+4)$$
$$5(4+3-5)-4(2+3-8)+2(6-5)-8(1+4-3).$$

N.B.—— $(3+5-2)$ may be regarded as the same thing as $-1(3+5-2)$ or $(-1) \times (3+5-2)$.

Or the $-$ may be regarded as indicating that all the quantities in the bracket are to be subtracted. Whichever way we think of it we get the same result, viz. :—

$$-(3+5-2) = -3-5+2.$$

28. Find the value of

$$3(5-6)-(4-5)-(6+4)$$
and of $\qquad 4(5-3+2)-(6-5+1)-2(1-2)$
and of $\qquad 5(8-5)-(7+2-3)+2(6-1).$

I F there be brackets within brackets, there is no difficulty in taking them away if we take away the *inner* brackets first. Thus :—

$$3[5+2\{4-2(7-3(2+3))\}]$$
$$= 3[5+2\{4-2(7-6-9)\}]$$
$$= 3[5+2\{4-14+12+18\}]$$
$$= 3[5+8-28+24+36]$$
$$= 15+24-84+72+108$$
$$= 135.$$

29. Simplify the following expressions :—

$$3\{1+2(3+4)\}+2\{1+2(3-4)\}$$
$$5\{3(2+1)+2(1-3)\}-2\{5(1-2)-3(4+2)\}$$
$$6\{3-(5-4)\}-2\{1-(4-2)\}-\{3+2(1-2)\}$$
$$5-3[5-3\{5-3(5-3)\}]$$
$$5-3[5-3(5-3)(5-3)].$$

W E can only add together or subtract numbers of things of the same kind: 3 and 2 will not make 5 if the 3 means three guineas and the 2 means two pounds. In the following exercises the *like* things must be collected together, and those that are unlike kept distinct. Ex. 30 exhibits the arrangement in addition, and Ex. 33 in subtraction.

30. John has 5 pears and 2 figs; Tom has 3 figs and 2 apples; Dick has 4 apples and 3 pears. What have they altogether?

$$\begin{array}{ll} \text{J. has} & 5 \text{ pears} + 2 \text{ figs} \\ \text{T. has} & 3 \text{ figs} \ \ + 2 \text{ apples} \\ \text{D. has} & 4 \text{ apples} + 3 \text{ pears} \\ \hline & 8 \text{ pears} + 5 \text{ figs} + 6 \text{ apples.} \end{array}$$

It might have been clearer if we had put it down in this way:—

$$\begin{array}{llll} \text{J. has} & 5 \text{ pears} + 2 \text{ figs} & & \\ \text{T. has} & & 3 \text{ figs} + 2 \text{ apples} \\ \text{D. has} & 3 \text{ pears} & & + 4 \text{ apples} \\ \hline & 8 \text{ pears} + & 5 \text{ figs} + & 6 \text{ apples.} \end{array}$$

31. John has 8 pears and 3 figs; Tom has 2 pears, 2 figs, and 2 apples; Dick has 5 apples and 3 pears. What have they altogether?

$$\begin{array}{l} 8\,p + 3\,f \\ 2\,p + 2\,f + 2\,a \\ 5\,a + 3\,p \\ \hline \end{array}$$

32. In a similar way add together:—

$$\begin{array}{ll} 3\,p + 2\,a \qquad\qquad & 3\,a + 5\,p + 2\,f \\ 5\,a + 3\,f & 4\,p + 3\,f \\ 4\,f + 2\,p & 4\,a + 3\,p \\ \hline \end{array}$$

33. John has 8 pears and 3 figs ; Tom has 2 pears, 2 figs, and 2 apples. How much richer is John than Tom?

We may arrange the subtraction thus :—

John has	$8\,p + 3\,f$
Tom has	$2\,p + 2\,f + 2\,a$
	$6\,p + 1\,f - 2\,a$

34. In a similar way :—

From	$3\,p + 2\,f$		$5\,p + 3\,f + 5\,a$
Take	$3\,p + 2\,a$		$8\,p + 4\,f$

From	$3\,f + 4\,a$		$4\,p + 3\,f + 2\,a$
Take	$4\,p + 3\,f$		$4\,f + 3\,a$

35. Add together all the answers in Ex. 34.

36. Add :—

$7\,p - 9\,a + 2\,f$	$3\,p - 2\,f + 3\,a$	$4\,p + 3\,f + 2\,a$
$3\,a - 5\,p + 6\,f$	$2\,p + 3\,f - 5\,a$	$-3\,p + 2\,f + 5\,a$
$4\,f + 6\,a - 2\,p$	$7\,p - 6\,f + 2\,a$	$2\,p - 5\,f + 3\,a$

$10\,p + 3\,a$	$3\,p - 5\,a$	$4\,a - 3\,f$
$5\,a - 7\,f$	$5\,f - 2\,p$	$4\,p + 5\,a$
$12\,f + 3\,p$	$2\,a - 7\,f$	$2\,f + 3\,p$
$6\,a - 7\,p$	$4\,p + 2\,a$	$4\,f - 3\,a$
$12\,f - 3\,a$	$3\,p - 4\,f$	$-6\,a - 7\,p$

37. Add together :—

$3\,f$	$-6\,f$	$7\,p$	$6\,p$	$3\,a$	$2\,a$
$-5\,a$	$7\,p$	$3\,a$	$-3\,a$	$-2\,p$	$-3\,p$
$7\,p$	$8\,a$	$4\,f$	$-5\,f$	$4\,f$	$6\,f$
$-9\,f$	$9\,f$	$2\,p$	$-2\,p$	$-3\,a$	$-5\,f$
$-11\,a$	$-5\,p$	$3\,a$	$7\,a$	$2\,p$	$4\,p$
$-13\,p$	$-4\,a$	$5\,f$	$5\,f$	$-3\,f$	$3\,a$

38. If s mean a score, and d a dozen, and h a half-dozen, what will be the value of

$$4s - 10d + 7h \qquad 5(s - h) + 2(3h - d)$$
$$6d - 5s + 3h \qquad 3(d + s) - 7(s + 2h)$$

39. Add together :—

$$
\begin{array}{ll}
3s - 4d & 5h - 3d + 2s \\
5d + 7h & 4h - 5s \\
2h - 5s & 3s - 7d \\
3s + 7d + 2h & 10d - 9h
\end{array}
$$

40.

$$
\begin{array}{lll}
\text{From} & 4s - 3h + 2d & 4s - 5d \\
\text{Take} & 2s - 5h - 4d & 3d - 2h \\[2mm]
\text{From} & 6s - 5h + 3d & 4h - 5d \\
\text{Take} & 2s + 5h + 3d & 5h - 4s
\end{array}
$$

41. Find the numerical values of the results in exercises 39 and 40; if h means a hundred, and s means seventy, and d means a dozen.

42. Add :—

$$
\begin{array}{lll}
5a - 2c & a - b & a + b + c \\
7a + 3b & b - c & b + c - a \\
2b + 4c & c - a & c + a - b \\
7a - 3b & a + b + c & a + b - c
\end{array}
$$

Note that instead of writing $1a$ and $-1a$ it is sufficient to write a and $-a$.

43. Add :—

$$
\begin{array}{ll}
3x - 5y + 2z & 4p - 3q + 2r \\
7x - 3y - z & 7p + 8q - 5r \\
-x + 2y + 3z & -10p - 4q + 4r
\end{array}
$$

44.

From	$3a + 5b - 4c$	$5x - 2y - 2z$
Take	$2a + 3b + 2c$	$3x + 2y + 2z$

From	$x - y + z$	$x + y - z$
Take	$x - y - z$	$x - y + z$

From	$a + b + c - d + e$	$a + b$
Take	$a - b - c + d + e$	$a - c$

From	$3x + 2y$	$a + b$	$a - b$	$3a$
Take	$3y - 2z$	$b + c$	$b - c$	$a + b + c$

From	$5x - y$	$4p + 3q - 5r$
Take	$3x - 2y - z$	$2p - 5q - 3r$

45. Simplify :—

$3\,(a + b) - 5\,(b + c) + 4\,(c + a)$.

$4\,(3a + 2b - 5c) + 5\,(2a - b + 3c) - 3\,(2b + 3c)$.

$2\,(x + 2y + 3z) - 3\,(y + 2z + 3x) + 4\,(z + 2x + 3y)$.

$1 - 2\{1 - 2(1 - x)\}$.

$1 - 2[3 - 4\{5 - 6(7 - x)\}]$.

$3\{5 + 4(x - 1)\} - 5\{3 - 2(x + 2)\}$.

$4\{5a - 4(b + c)\} + 3\{2(a + b) - 3c\}$.

THE teacher will now explain how, just as the sum of x and y can only be put down as $x + y$ (unless we know the value of x and y), so the product of the same numbers must be put down as $x \times y$, or more briefly xy (the sign of multiplication understood between the x and the y). So, if x be multiplied by itself, the product will be written xx. It must be observed, in performing addition and subtraction, that x and xx and xxx are *unlike* quantities as much as x and y and z are. Similarly, ab and ac, and aab and abb are unlike, and will enter separately into the result.

46. Add :—

$2ab + 3bc - 5ac$	$2xxx + 3xx + 5x$
$4aa - 5ab - 3bc$	$2xx - 5x + 17$
$9bb - 9ab + 5ac$	$xxx - 3x - 12$

47. Simplify the following expressions by removing the brackets :—

$a (b - c) + b (c - a) + c (a - b)$.

$a (x + y) - x (a + y) + y (a + x)$.

$a (a + b + c) - aa - b (a + c)$.

$x (x - y + z) + y (y - z + x) + z(z - x + y)$.

$a (bb - ac) + b (cc - ab) + c (aa - bc)$.

$a (a - b + c) - b (a - b + c) + c (a - b + c)$.

$a (aa + ab + bb) - b (aa + ab + bb)$.

$xx (y - z) + yz (x - y) - xy (x + z)$.

THE order of the factors in multiplication being indifferent, we have—

$$3a \times 5b = 3 \times a \times 5 \times b$$
$$= 3 \times 5 \times a \times b$$
$$= 15ab$$

Similarly, $3a \times 5a = 15aa$.

48. Simplify the following expressions :—

$3a (2b - 5c) + 2b (3c - 4a) + 2c (5a - 2b)$.

$3x (7x + 5) - 7 (3xx + 2x + 3) + 21$.

$3x (xx - yz) - 5y (yy - xz) + 2z (zz - xy)$.

$5a (3b + 2c - 4d) + 3b (4c - d - 5a) - 3d (3a - b + c)$.

$x[x\{x(x - a) + bb\} + ccc] + dddd$.

IN the expression $(3a - 2b) (x + y + z)$ the brackets tell us that the whole of $x + y + z$ is to be multiplied by the whole of $3a - b$. We may first multiply $x + y + z$ by $3a$, and then multiply it by $- 2b$, and thus get the complete result—

$$3ax + 3ay + 3az - 2bx - 2by - 2bz.$$

49. Simplify :—

$$(a + b) (x + y) + (a - b) (x - y).$$
$$(a + b) (a + b) + (a + b) (a - b).$$
$$(x + 3) (xx - 3x + 9) + 9 (x - 3).$$

WHEN we have to multiply by a series of terms, it is often convenient to set down in separate lines the result of multiplying by the several terms, and then add the lines together. We may arrange the work as in the following example :—

50. Multiply $x + y - z$ by $x - y + z$:—

$$x + y - z$$
$$x - y + z$$

Top line × x	$xx + xy - xz$
„ × $(-y)$	$- xy - yy + yz$
„ × z	$xz + yz - zz$
adding	$xx \quad - yy + 2yz - zz.$

51. Multiply :—

$x + a$ by $x + b.$
$xx - 3x + 5$ by $3x + 2.$
$xx + 6x + 10$ by $3x - 5.$
$xxx - 2xx + 4x - 8$ by $x + 2.$
$xx + xy + yy$ by $x - y.$
$xx + xy + yy$ by $xx - xy + yy.$

52. Multiply :—

$4aa + bb + cc + 2ab + bc - 2ca$ by $2a - b + c.$
$5aa + 7a - 12$ by $3a + 5.$
$4aa - 6a + 5$ by $4aa + 6a + 5.$

53. Multiply $2x + 3$ by itself.
Multiply $xx - 2xy + 4yy$ by itself.
Multiply $xx + yy + zz - yz - zx - xy$ by $x + y + z.$

54. Simplify :—

$6 - 2\left(3 - x\right) - 3\left(2 - x\right) + \left(3 - x\right)\left(2 - x\right).$

$\left(x + 5\right)\left(x - 3\right) - 2(x - 7).$

$\left(3x + 2\right)\left(2x + 3\right) - 6\left(x + 1\right)\left(x + 1\right).$

$\left(5x - 3\right)\left(3x + 5\right) - 15\left(x + 1\right)\left(x - 1\right).$

$\left(x + 3\right)\left(x + 3\right) + \left(x + 4\right)\left(x + 4\right) - \left(x + 5\right)\left(x + 5\right).$

$\left(x + 3\right)\left(x - 3\right) + \left(x + 4\right)\left(x - 4\right) - \left(x + 5\right)\left(x - 5\right).$

55. Find the continued product :—

$$\left(a + b + c\right)\left(a - b + c\right)\left(a + b - c\right)\left(a - b - c\right);$$

and the continued product

$$\left(xxxx + yyyy\right)\left(xx + yy\right)\left(x + y\right)\left(x - y\right).$$

TO save trouble it is usual to write x^2, x^4, x^8, instead of xx, $xxxx$, $xxxxxxxx$. If the pupil will always think of what these expressions x^2, x^4, &c., stand for, there will be no difficulty in multiplying them together as in the next example. Similarly we may write $(x+y)^2$ and $(x+y)^3$ instead of $(x+y)(x+y)$ and $(x+y)(x+y)(x+y)$, and so on.

56. Multiply $5x^3$ by $2x^4$.

That is, $5xxx \times 2xxxx$

$$= 10xxxxxxx$$

$$= 10x^7.$$

57. Perform the following multiplications :—

$x^2 \times x^3$	$3x^2 \times 2x^3$	$4x^3 \times 5x^3$
$x^3 \times x^4$	$2x^4 \times x^2$	$4x^4 \times 4x^4$
$3a^3 \times 3a^3$	$5a^3 \times a$	$x^7 \times x$
$3x^2y^3 \times 2x^3y^2$	$ax^3 \times a^4x$	$a^5 \times ax^6$
$a^6x^6 \times 2a^2x^4$	$xyz \times xy^2z^3$	$5a^5 \times 6a^6$
$xy \times xy \times xy$		$x^3y^3 \times x^2y^2 \times xy$

58. Write the following quantities without brackets :—

$(3a)^2$ $(4ab)^2$ $(2x)^3$ $(5x^2y)^2$ $(3x)^4$ $(a-b)^2$
$(x+y)^2$ $(x+3)^2$ $(2x-3)^2$ $(5a+4b)^2$ $(2x-1)^2$
$(a+b)^3$ $(x-y)^3$ $(x+1)^3$ $(x^2-x+1)^2$.

59. Multiply :—

$2x+3$ by $x-3$ 　　　　x^2-4 by x^2+4
$3x+5$ by $3x-5$ 　　　　x^2-5 by $2x-3$
a^2-7a+3 by $a-4$
x^2+x+1 by x^2-x+1
$5a^2+4a+3$ by $3a^2+4a-5$
$13m^2-5mn+12n^2$ by $12m^2-5mn-13n^2$
x^4-x^3-x+1 by x^2+x+1
$a^4+2a^3+8a+16$ by a^2-2a+4.

60. Simplify :—

$$(2x+3y)^2+(2x-3y)^2.$$
$$(2x+3y)^2+(3x-2y)^2.$$
$$(x+y)^3-3xy\,(x+y).$$
$$(x+y+z)^3-3\,(xy+yz+zx)\,(x+y+z).$$
$$(a+b)^2-(b+c)^2+(c+d)^2-(d+a)^2.$$
$$(5a+3b)^2+16\,(3a+b)^2-(13a+5b)^2.$$
$$(5a-4c)^2+9\,(4a-c)^2-(13a-5c)^2.$$
$$(5x+3y-4z)^2+(12x+4y-3z)^2-(13x+5y-5z)^2.$$

61. Simplify :—

$$(x-3)^2-2\,(x-3)\,(x+2)+(x+2)^2.$$
$$(x^2+y^2)^2-(2xy)^2-(x^2-y^2)^2.$$
$$(a^3-3ab^2)^2+(3a^2b-b^3)^2-(a^2+b^2)^3.$$
$$(x^5-10x^3+5x)^2+(5x^4-10x^2+1)^2-(x^2+1)^5.$$
$$(a-b)^3+(b-c)^3+(c-a)^3-3(b-c)\,(c-a)\,(a-b).$$

DIVISION may be taught here if it be thought fit; but it may be better to press on to equations, and to teach division immediately before fractions. If it be regarded as the undoing of multiplication, it presents no difficulty to those who have learned to do multiplication intelligently.

62. Exercises in Division :—

$6x \div 2x.$ $6x^2 \div 2x.$ $6xy \div 2x.$

$6xy \div 3y.$ $-6x^2y^2 \div x^2.$ $6x^2y^2 \div 3xy.$

$a^3b^2c \div a.$ $-a^3b^2c \div abc.$ $4pqr \div 2pq.$

$a^3b^2c \div a^2b.$ $a^3b^2c \div ab^2.$ $x^2 \div (-x).$

$-12a^4b^3c^2 \div 3abc.$ $12a^4b^3c^2 \div 4a^2b^2c^2.$

$(2x^2 + 3xy) \div x.$ $(6xy + 9y^2) \div 3y.$

$(a^3b - 2a^2b^2 + ab^3) \div ab.$ $(a^3 - 3a^2b) \div (-a^2).$

THE process of dividing by a series of terms ought to be explained on the black board, and illustrated by the next example.

63. Divide :—

$$a^3 + 3a^2x - 4ax^2 - 12x^3 \text{ by } a - 2x.$$

$$a - 2x \,)\; a^3 + 3a^2x - \;\;4ax^2 - 12x^3 \,(\; a^2 + 5ax + 6x^2$$
$$\underline{a^3 - 2a^2x}$$
$$5a^2x - \;\;4ax^2$$
$$\underline{5a^2x - 10ax^2}$$
$$6ax^2 - 12x^3$$
$$\underline{6ax^2 - 12x^3}$$

64. Divide :—

$$x^2 - 5x + 4 \text{ by } x - 4.$$
$$a^2 - 4a + 4 \text{ by } a - 2.$$
$$a^3 - 3a^2 + 2 \text{ by } a - 1.$$
$$(x - a)(x - b) - (y - a)(y - b) \text{ by } x - y.$$
$$x^2(a - b) - a^2(x - b) \text{ by } x - a.$$
$$2x^3 - x^2 + 3 \text{ by } x + 1.$$
$$3x^4 - 20x^2 - 22x + 3 \text{ by } x - 3.$$
$$60(a^4 + 1) + 91a(a^2 - 1) \text{ by } 12a^2 - 13a + 5.$$

65. Find the quotients of the following :—

$(a^3 - 3a^2x - 4ax^2 + 12x^3) \div (a - 2x)$.

$(x^4 - y^4) \div (x^2 - y^2)$. $(m^4 - n^4) \div (m^2 + n^2)$.

$(x^4 - y^4) \div (x - y)$. $(x^5 + y^5) \div (x + y)$.

$(a^3 + b^3 + c^3 - 3abc) \div (a + b + c)$.

$(a^6 - 3a^4x^2 + 3a^2x^4 - x^6) \div (a^3 - 3a^2x + 3ax^2 - x^3)$.

$(x^5 - ax^4 + bx^3 - bx^2 + ax - 1) \div (x - 1)$.

66. Find the remainder when the following operations of division are performed :—

$$(x^3 - 5x^2 + 2x + 5) \div (x - 1).$$
$$(x^3 + x^2 + 1) \div (x + 2).$$
$$(x^4 - 3x^2 + 1) \div (x - 3).$$
$$x^4 \div (x - 3).$$

67. Divide :—

$(m + 1)^2 - (n + 1)^2$ by $m - n$, and $(a^5 - 10a^3b^2 + 5ab^4)^2 + (5a^4b - 10a^2b^3 + b^5)^2$ by $(a^3 - 3ab^2)^2 + (3a^2b - b^3)^2$.

68. If $a = 4$, $b = 3$, $c = 2$, $d = 1$, $m = 9$, $n = 8$, $r = 0$, find the value of each of the following expressions :—

$$a - 3\{b - 2(c - d)\}$$
$$m - 8[n - 7\{a - 2(b - c)\}]$$
$$(a + m)(b + n + c) + (a + c - d)(a - m)$$
$$+ (a + n)(r - m - b)$$
$$a^2 + b^2 + c^2 - bc - ca - ab$$
$$m^2 + n^2 + r^2 - 2mn - 2mr - 2nr$$

$(n + c)^2 - 2(m - c)^2$ $\qquad$ $(m - c)^2 - 2(a + d)^2$

$(a - m)^3 + (b + n)^2$ $\qquad$ $a^2c^3 - (b + c)^3$

$b^4 - 5c^4$ $\qquad$ $(c + d)^3 - (b + c)^2$

$(a^2 - nc)(b + d) + (b^2 - md)(c + a) + (c^2 - ad)(m + n)$

$(a^3 - nb^2)(a - b - c) + (b^3 - mc^2)(c - d) + (c^3 - md^2)(a - b)$

69. Find the value of

$x^2 + y^2 - z^2$ when $x = 3$, $y = 4$, $z = 5$.
also when $x = 5$, $y = 12$, $z = 13$.
also when $x = 15$, $y = 8$, $z = 17$.

70. Find the value of

$x^2 - 12x + 35$ when $x = 5$.
also when $x = 6$.
also when $x = 7$.

71. Find the value of

$x^4 - 15x^2 + 10x + 24$ when $x = -1$.
also when $x = 2$.
· also when $x = 3$.
also when $x = -4$.
also when $x = 0$.

72. Examine which of the following statements are true and which are false if $x = 2$:—

$2x + 3 = 5$	$2x - 3 = 1$
$2x + 3 = 7$	$2x - 3 = x + 1$
$2x + 3 = 9$	$x + 3 = 15 - 2x.$

73. Which of them are true if $x = 3$?

74. Which of them are true if $x = 4$?

75. Examine which of the following statements are true when $x = 2$ or 3 or 5 :—

$x^2 + 4 = 4x$	$x^2 + 10 = 7x$
$x^2 + 6 = 5x$	$x^2 + 15 = 8x$
$x^2 + 9 = 6x$	$x^2 + 25 = 10x$

$$x(x^2 + 31) = 10(x^2 + 3).$$

76. If $5x = 60$ what must be the value of x?

If $7y = 91$ what must be the value of y?

If $3z = -12$ what must be the value of z?

If $-3x = 12$ what must be the value of x?

If $5x = 0$ what is x?

If $4z = 21$ what is z?

If $20y = 1$ what is y?

. If $15z = -3$ what is z?

If $7x = -20$ what is x?

If $9p = 9$ what is p?

THE teacher will next explain how any term may be made to disappear in either member of an equation by adding the complementary term to both members. Thus, if we have the equation

$$3x + 5y = 2z,$$

adding $-5y$ to both members we get

$$3x = 2z - 5y,$$

where $5y$ has disappeared from the first member, and the complementary term $-5y$ has appeared in the second member. Thus in a simple equation all the terms involving an unknown quantity x may be made to disappear from one member, and all the terms involving only known quantities from the other.

77. Find x when $3x + 5 = 33 - x$. We shall make $-x$ disappear from the second member, and 5 from the first, by adding to both members the complementary terms, x and -5. Thus we get

$$3x + x = 33 - 5,$$
$$\text{or} \quad 4x = 28,$$

whence it is plain that $x = 7$.

78. Find x from each of the following equations :—

$3x - 7 = 2x + 1.$

$5x - 3 = 4x + 3.$

$17 - 3x = 20 - 4x.$

$3x + 1 = x + 9.$

$5x + 1 = 2x + 10.$

$2x - 5 + 3x - 7 = 4x + 1.$

$5x - 7 - 3x = 21 - 2x.$

$4x - 5 + 2x - 11 = 84 - 4x.$

79. Find x from each of the following equations :—

$3(x - 5) + 2(x - 3) = 4.$

$5(x - 7) + 3(x - 3) = 4(x - 4).$

$3(x + 1) + 4(x + 2) = 5(x + 3).$

$13(x + 4) - 12(x + 3) = 5(x - 4).$

$5(x - 1) + 24x = 13(2x + 1).$

$5(x - 2) + 48(x - 4) = 13(2x - 1).$

$(x - 1)(x - 2) = (x - 3)(x - 4).$

80. Find x from each of the following equations :—

$(5x + 3)^2 - (3x - 1)^2 = 16(x + 1)^2.$

$(5x - 2)^2 - (3x - 4)^2 = 16x^2.$

$(2x - 3)(3x - 2) = 6(x - 2)^2 + 4.$

$(13x - 21)^2 = 16(3x - 5)^2 + (5x - 7)^2.$

$2(3x - 2) = 11(11 - 4x).$

$3(x + 2) = 2(x - 3).$

$5 - 17x = 2 + 13x.$

$(4 - x)(x - 2) + x^2 = 0.$

AN equation may be cleared of fractions by multiplying both members of it by a multiple of all the denominators. It is supposed that the student is already so familiar with arithmetical fractions that he will find no difficulty here. If this is not the case, it will be necessary to turn aside and teach the *theory of fractions,* following the outline given on pages 41-44.

81. ·Solve the equation
$$\frac{x+1}{20} + \frac{x+2}{15} = \frac{x+3}{12}.$$
[ultiplying throughout by 60 we get
$$3(x+1) + 4(x+2) = 5(x+3),$$
nd we can then proceed as in former examples.

82. Solve the following equations :—

$$\frac{x}{2} + \frac{x}{3} + \frac{x}{4} = 22 + \frac{x}{6}.$$

$$\frac{x-5}{2} + \frac{x-3}{6} = \frac{x-7}{4}.$$

$$\frac{x+1}{5} + \frac{x+3}{7} = \frac{x+2}{3}.$$

$$\frac{1}{5}(7x+4) - x = \frac{1}{2}(3x-5).$$

$$\frac{x+1}{15} + \frac{x}{20} = \frac{x+2}{12}.$$

$$\frac{x}{65} + \frac{x-7}{156} = \frac{x+1}{60}.$$

$$\frac{3}{16}(x+1) + \frac{1}{15}(7x-4) - \frac{1}{20}(7x+1) = 2.$$

$$\frac{x+6}{4} + \frac{3x-16}{12} = \frac{25}{6}.$$

$$\frac{x+1}{2x} + \frac{3x+4}{3} = x+2.$$

$$\frac{2}{3x} + \frac{3}{2x} = 13.$$

$$(10x-1)^2 = (8x+3)^2 + (6x-6)^2.$$
$$(8x-1)^2 + (15x+5)^2 = (17x+4)^2.$$
$$(5x-3)^2 = (2x+7)(8x-17) + (3x-4)^2.$$

IN the equations of Exercise 83, x has to be found in terms of the quantities a, b, c, &c. All these latter, being understood to represent known quantities, must be treated just as the numerals of the previous equations, and they will generally appear in the final answer.

83. Find x from the following equations :—

$2a - x = x + 2b.$

$5(x - a) + 3(x - b) = 3(a - b).$

$4(x - a) + 3(x - b) - 5(x - c) = x - 4a - 2b + 5c.$

$3(x + 2a) - 5(x - b) + x = 2(3a + 3b - x).$

$5(2x - c + a) + 3(x + b + c) = 4(x + a + c) + a + 3b.$

$\dfrac{x + b}{3} + \dfrac{x - a}{2} = \dfrac{x - 5b}{3} + x - 2a.$

$\dfrac{a - x}{2} + \dfrac{x - b}{3} + \dfrac{x - c}{4} = \dfrac{10a - 3x + c}{12}.$

$m(x - m) + n(x - n) = 2mn.$

$3a(x - a) + 2b(x - b) = 5ab.$

$(a - b)^2 + 4(x - c)(x - d) = (c - d)^2 + 4(x - a)(x - b).$

IN each of the following questions a statement is made respecting some unknown number. If we put x to represent the unknown number, we can write down the statement in algebraical symbols. That statement is an equation which we can solve. Thus we find the value of x, the unknown number.

84. A certain number increased by 2 and multiplied by 3 comes to 27. Find the number.

Let x represent the number; increase it by 2 and we get $x + 2$; multiply by 3 and we get $3(x + 2)$, and the statement is $3(x + 2) = 27$, from which equation we get $x = 7$.

85. A certain number multiplied by 3 and then in-creased by 2 comes to 26. Find it.

86. There are a certain number of boys in a school, and the same number of girls. 30 girls leave and 40 new boys come, and then the boys are twice as many as the girls. How many were there at first ?

87. Tom is 4 times as old as John : in 8 years Tom will be twice as old as John. Find their ages.

Let x represent John's age now ; then $4x$ is Tom's age. In 8 years they will be $x+8$ and $4x+8$, then write down the equation.

88. Find a number such that to multiply it. by 5 and add 3 gives the same as to multiply it by 7 and subtract 4.

89. Find a number such that to multiply it by 4 and add 3 gives the same as to add 4 and then multiply by 3.

90. Find a number such that to multiply it by 4 and add 2 is the same as to add 4 and then multiply by 2.

91. Find three consecutive numbers which added together will come to 15.

92. Find four consecutive numbers which added together will come to 34.

93. The number of boys who went in for an examination was one more than the number of girls. One-sixth of the boys and one-fifth of the girls failed to pass. Of those that passed there were three more boys than girls. How many of each went in for the examination ?

94. John has three times as many marbles as Tom. If Tom gives John 15, John will then have six times as many as Tom. How many has each ?

c

95. If each side of a square room were increased by 1 foot, the area would be increased by 41 square feet. Find the dimensions of the room.

96. Divide 34 marbles between two children so that one may have 6 more than the other.

97. Divide 46 marbles between John and Tom, so that John's share may be 5 less than twice Tom's.

98. A school consists of 3 classes : the 1st contains 2 less than half the school, the 2d contains 4 less than one-third of the school, and the 3d contains 1 less than a quarter of the school. How many are there in each class ?

EVEN in such simple problems as the preceding, the beginner will often find it easier (though longer) to use more than one unknown quantity. It is well, therefore, at once to proceed to the solution of simultaneous equations.

99. Find x and y when

$$\left. \begin{array}{l} 2x + 9y = 35. \\ 3x + 2y = 18. \end{array} \right\}$$

Multiplying the first equation by 3 and the second by 2, so as to make each begin with $6x$,

$$6x + 27y = 105.$$
$$6x + 4y = 36.$$

Subtracting $\qquad 23y = 69.$

whence $\qquad\qquad y = 3.$

Writing 3 for y, in the first of the given equations, we get —

$$2x + 27 = 35.$$
$$2x = 8.$$
$$x = 4.$$

thus the values of x and y are both found.

100. Solve the following simultaneous equations :—

$$\left.\begin{array}{l} 2x - 5y = 5 \\ 3x + 2y = 36 \end{array}\right\} \qquad \left.\begin{array}{l} 5x - 4y = 8 \\ 4x - 5y = 1 \end{array}\right\} \qquad \left.\begin{array}{l} 9x - 4y = 8 \\ 2x - y = 1 \end{array}\right\}$$

$$\left.\begin{array}{l} 5x - 4y = 9 \\ x - y = 1 \end{array}\right\} \qquad \left.\begin{array}{l} 5x - 3y = 16 \\ x + y = 8 \end{array}\right\} \qquad \left.\begin{array}{l} 7x - 6y = 13 \\ 6x - 7y = 0 \end{array}\right\}$$

$$\left.\begin{array}{l} 7x - 5y = 3 \\ 5x - 2y = 10 \end{array}\right\} \qquad \left.\begin{array}{l} 3x - 2y = 11 \\ 2x + 3y = 16 \end{array}\right\} \qquad \left.\begin{array}{l} x + y = 0 \\ 5x - 6y = 44 \end{array}\right\}$$

$$\left.\begin{array}{l} x + y = 31 \\ x - y = 21 \end{array}\right\} \qquad \left.\begin{array}{l} 3x + 2y - 5 = 0 \\ x + 5y - 6 = 0 \end{array}\right\} \qquad \left.\begin{array}{l} 3x + y = 17 \\ 5x - 2y = 10 \end{array}\right\}$$

101.

$$\left.\begin{array}{l} 101x - 24y = 63 \\ 103x - 28y = 29 \end{array}\right\} \qquad \left.\begin{array}{l} 54x - 121y = 15 \\ 36x - 77y = 21 \end{array}\right\}$$

$$\left.\begin{array}{l} 3(x + 11) + 5(y - 4) = 30(x - 7) \\ 3(x + 5) - 7(y - 7) = 21(3y - x) \end{array}\right\}$$

$$\left.\begin{array}{l} \dfrac{x + 1}{3} + \dfrac{2y - 5}{5} = \dfrac{2}{15} \\ 11x + 10y = 4 \end{array}\right\} \qquad \left.\begin{array}{l} \dfrac{x - 3}{4} + \dfrac{y - 2}{5} = 0 \\ x - y = 1. \end{array}\right\}$$

$$\left.\begin{array}{l} \tfrac{1}{2}(x + 1) + \tfrac{1}{4}(y + 1) = 3 \\ 2x - y = 3 \end{array}\right\}$$

$$\left.\begin{array}{l} \tfrac{1}{5}(7 + x) - \tfrac{1}{4}(2x - y) = 3y - 5 \\ 3(5y - 7) + 4x - 3 = 6(18 - 5x) \end{array}\right\}$$

$$\left.\begin{array}{l} 2x - \dfrac{y - 3}{5} = 4 \\ 3y + \dfrac{x - 2}{3} = 9 \end{array}\right\} \qquad \left.\begin{array}{l} \dfrac{5x}{y + 1} = 2 \\ \dfrac{3y}{x + 1} = 4 \end{array}\right\}$$

T HE student will find that the process of solving three simultaneous equations with three unknown quantities introduces no new difficulty, though the operation is often long. The following example will illustrate the explanation, which the teacher will give from the black-board :—

102. Find $x\ y\ z$ from the equations

$$\left.\begin{array}{l} 3x + 2y - 5z = 8. \\ 2x - 5y + 3z = -1. \\ 4x + y - 7z = 5. \end{array}\right\}$$

Multiplying the first equation by 2, and the second by 3, and subtracting, we get—

$$19y - 19z = 19, \text{ or } y - z = 1.$$

Multiplying the second by 2, and subtracting it from the third we get—

$$11y - 13z = 7.$$

We have now formed two equations, involving only y and z. Solving them together, as in previous examples, we find—

$$y = 3 \qquad z = 2.$$

And writing these values in the first equation, we get—

$$3x + 6 - 10 = 8$$
$$\text{whence} \qquad x = 4.$$

103. Solve the following simultaneous equations :—

$$\left.\begin{array}{l} 2x - y + z = 1 \\ x + y + z = 4 \\ 3x + 2y - 5z = 2 \end{array}\right\} \qquad \left.\begin{array}{l} 3x + 5y - 2z = 9 \\ 4x - 7y + 3z = 13 \\ 3x + 4y - 5z = -8 \end{array}\right\}$$

$$\left.\begin{array}{l} y + z = 12 \\ z + x = 11 \\ x + y = 9 \end{array}\right\} \qquad \left.\begin{array}{l} x + y + z = 35 \\ x - z = 2 \\ y - z = 3 \end{array}\right\}$$

104. John and Tom together have £50, James and Tom have £40, and John and James have £30. How much has each ?

105. John is 5 years older than Tom, Tom is a year older than James, and their ages added together come to 34 years. Find the ages.

106. Jane and Ann and Mary have 15 shillings amongst them, but Jane has twice as much as Ann, and Ann has a shilling more than Mary. How much has each?

107. What number is that the triple of which is as much above 40 as its half is below 51?

108. Find two numbers in the ratio of 8 : 5 whose difference shall be 21.

109. Find two numbers whose sum is 8 times their difference, and 3 times the lesser exceeds twice the greater by 6.

110. John is twice as old as Tom, and in 4 years he will be twice as old as Dick. Six years ago Tom was twice as old as Dick. Find their ages.

111. Find two numbers whose sum is 40 and difference 6.

112. The difference of two numbers is 5, and twice the lesser one exceeds the greater by 2. Find them.

113. How much tea at 4s. per lb. must be mixed with 20 lbs. at 3s. and 10 lbs. at 2s. 6d., so that the mixture may be worth 3s. 6d. per lb.?

114. A woman buys eggs at 1d. each, she breaks 6 of them, and sells the rest at 5 farthings each, making a total profit of 6d. How many did she buy?

115. If 3 men and 5 boys earn 30 shillings a day, and 4 men and 2 boys earn 26 shillings a day, what are the wages of each?

116. If a man earns in a day 4 shillings more than a boy, and 7 men and 5 boys earn 40 shillings a day, what are the wages of each ?

117. Six pennies and 15 halfpennies weigh 5 ounces, 30 pennies and 30 halfpennies weigh 16 ounces, what are the weights of a penny and a halfpenny ?

118. I paid 15 shillings in fourpenny and threepenny pieces. If there were 54 coins altogether, how many of each sort ?

119. I paid 7 shillings in sixpences, fourpences, and threepences. The number of fourpences was the same as the number of sixpences, and the fourpences and threepences were equal in value. How many were paid of each ?

120. A train starts from London for Liverpool going 37 miles an hour, at the same time another starts from Liverpool for London at 30 miles an hour. If the distance between Liverpool and London be 201 miles, after how long will they meet ?

121. Three pennies weigh an ounce, and five halfpennies weigh an ounce. If £1 worth of pennies and halfpennies weigh 87 ounces, how many are there of each ?

122. A man rows down a river at 8 miles an hour, and returns at 5 miles an hour, the whole journey occupying 6½ hours. How far did he go ?

123. If John gives Tom 3d., Tom will have twice as much as John, but if Tom gives John 2d., John will have three times as much as Tom. How much has each ?

GREATEST COMMON MEASURE AND LEAST COMMON MULTIPLE.

$\mathbf{F}$ACTORS of a given quantity are quantities whose continued product is equal to the given quantity. Thus x, x, y, are factors of x^2y, and 2, 3, 5, are factors of 30.

A prime factor is a quantity which cannot itself be expressed as the product of two other factors.

When quantities are resolved into their prime factors, we can write down at sight their G.C.M. (that is, the greatest quantity which is a factor or measure of *all* of them) and their L.C.M. (that is, the least quantity which is a multiple of all of them).

For the G.C.M. is the product of any factors which are common to *all* the quantities, and the L.C.M. is the product of all the different factors which occur in any of them, each factor being repeated the greatest number of times that it is repeated in any of the quantities.

For example, $\qquad$ $900 = 2.2.3.3.5.5,$
$$840 = 2.2.2.3.5.7;$$
$\therefore$ the G.C.M. of 900 and 840 is $2.2.3.5 = 60$
and their L.C.M. is $\quad 2.2.2.3.3.5.5.7 = 12600.$

Similarly, $\qquad$ G.C.M. of $6a^2bc^2$ and $4abc^3 = 2abc^2$;
and their $\qquad$ L.C.M. is $\qquad = 12a^2bc^3.$

124. Find the G.C.M. and L.C.M.

Of 60 and 66. Of 24 and 60. Of 63 and 49. Of 370 and 333. Of 1000 and 625. Of 1000 and 1024. Of $6a^2b^3$ and $8a^3b^2$. Of a^2bc, ab^2c, and abc^2. Of xy^2z and y^3z^3. Of mn and nr. Of lmr, mnr, and lnr. Of $24yz$, $36xz$, and $60xy$. Of ab and abc. Of x^2 and $2x$. Of x^3 and x^5.

125. The product of any two quantities is equal to the product of their G.C.M. and L.C.M. Illustrate this statement by examples, both arithmetical and algebraical.

IF an algebraical expression consists of more than one term,* we cannot generally recognise its factors at sight. The G.C.M. of two such quantities can, however, generally be found by a process analogous to the process of finding the G.C.M. in arithmetic, by dividing one quantity by the other, making the remainder into a new divisor, and the previous divisor into a new dividend, and repeating the process until there is no remainder. The last divisor is then the G.C.M. The chief point in which the algebraical process differs from the arithmetical, is that simple factors (*i.e.*, factors consisting of *one term*, and therefore easily recognised at sight) are to be divided out of the two given quantities, and the G.C.M. of these simple factors (if any) separately noted, and finally multiplied into the common measure obtained by the process of division. All simple factors are likewise to be divided out of the remainders which occur in the process of division, before those remainders are treated as new divisors. The explanation of this method belongs to a later stage in algebra, but it may be convenient for the student to learn here to apply it in simple cases.

When the G.C.M. of two quantities is found, their L.C.M. can always be determined by the principle enunciated in Ex. 125.

126. Find the G.C.M. and L.C.M. of $x^2 - 4x + 3$ and $x^2 - 3x + 2$, and of $a^3 - 3a^2b + 3ab^2 - b^3$ and $a^2 - 4ab + 3b^2$.

$$x^2 - 4x + 3 \;)\; x^2 - 3x + 2 \;(\; 1$$
$$\underline{x^2 - 4x + 3}$$
$$x - 1) \; x^2 - 4x + 3 \;(\; x - 3$$
$$\underline{x^2 - x}$$
$$-3x + 3$$
$$\underline{-3x + 3}$$

$\therefore$ The G.C.M. is $x - 3$, and the L.C.M. is then found to be $x^3 - 6x^2 + 11x - 6$.

---

* Those parts of an algebraical expression which are connected by the sign + or − are called *terms*, while those parts *which are connected* by the sign × are called *factors*.

$$a^2 - 4ab + 3b^2) a^3 - 3a^2b + 3ab^2 - b^3 (a + b$$
$$\underline{a^3 - 4a^2b + 3ab^2}$$
$$\underline{a^2b \qquad\qquad - b^3}$$
$$a^2b - 4ab^2 + 3b^3$$
$$\overline{\qquad 4ab^2 - 4b^3}$$

Out of this remainder we divide the simple factor $4b^2$, and thus get $a - b$, and proceed—

$$a - b) a^2 - 4ab + 3b^2 (a - 3b$$
$$\underline{a^2 - ab}$$
$$- 3ab + 3b^2$$
$$- 3ab + 3b^2$$

$\therefore$ The G.C.M. is $a - b$, and the L.C.M. is then found to be $a^4 - 6a^3b + 12a^2b^2 - 10ab^3 + 3b^4$.

127. Find the G.C.M. and L.C.M.

Of $x^2 - 4x + 4$ and $x^2 - 3x + 2$.

Of $x^2 - 4x + 3$ and $x^2 - 5x + 4$.

Of $p^2 - 4pq + 3q^2$ and $p^2 - 5pq + 4q^2$.

Of $3m^2 + 4m + 1$ and $6m^2 + 7m + 1$.

Of $a^2 - b^2$ and $a^3 - b^3$.

Of $a^3 + b^3$ and $a^5 + b^5$.

Of $a^4 - a^2b^2$ and $a^3b + a^2b^2$.

Of $x^3 - 6x^2y + 12xy^2 - 8y^3$ and $x^4 - 8x^2y^2 + 16y^4$.

FRACTIONS.

THE theory of fractions is the same for arithmetic and algebra, and the pupil who has done his arithmetic well needs not any new investigation of the properties of fractions here. Nevertheless, the introduction of algebraical symbols adds so much to the conciseness with which the theory of fractions can be enunciated, that it seems well to give here an abstract of it.

(i.) Definition. If a unit be divided into D equal parts, N such parts make the fraction $\dfrac{N}{D}$.

(ii.) N is called the numerator, because it tells the number of parts in the fraction. D is called the denominator, because it names those parts, by showing how many of them would make up a unit. It follows that

$$\frac{N}{1} = N, \text{ and that } \frac{N}{N} = 1.$$

(iii.) The fraction $\dfrac{mN}{D}$ is m times as great as $\dfrac{N}{D}$, because it contains m times as many parts, and the parts are of the same denomination. In other words,

$$\frac{mN}{D} = \frac{N}{D} \times m.$$

or *a fraction is multiplied by multiplying the numerator.*

(iv.) The fraction $\dfrac{N}{mD}$ is the mth part of the fraction $\dfrac{N}{D}$, because it contains the same number of parts, but each part m times as small, the unit having been divided into m times as many parts as before. In other words,

$$\frac{N}{mD} = \frac{N}{D} \div m.$$

or *a fraction is divided by multiplying the denominator.*

(v.) The fraction $\dfrac{mN}{mD}$ is equal to $\dfrac{N}{D}$, because (by iii. and iv.) $\dfrac{N}{D}$ has been both multiplied and divided by m to produce

$$\frac{mN}{mD}.$$

In other words, *the value of a fraction is not altered if the numerator and denominator be both multiplied by the same number.*

Conversely *the value of a fraction is not altered if the numerator and denominator be both divided by the same number.*

(vi.) It follows that $\dfrac{N}{D} \times D = \dfrac{DN}{D} = \dfrac{N}{1} = N.$

In other words, *a fraction multiplied by the number in the denominator produces the number in the numerator.*

(vii.) Since division is the undoing of multiplication,

$$\dfrac{N}{D} = \dfrac{N}{D} \times D \div D.$$

and therefore by (vi.)

$$= N \div D.$$

(viii.) Multiplication of fractions. Assuming that the order of the factors in continued multiplication is indifferent we have :—

$$\dfrac{N}{D} \times \dfrac{n}{d} = \dfrac{N}{D} \times \dfrac{n}{d} \times d \div d$$

$$= \dfrac{N}{D} \times n \div d \quad \text{by (vi.)}$$

$$= \dfrac{nN}{dD} \text{ by (iii.) and (iv.)}$$

In other words, *two fractions are multiplied together by multiplying the two numerators for a new numerator, and the two denominators for a new denominator.*

(ix.) $\dfrac{N}{D} \times \dfrac{D}{N} = \dfrac{ND}{ND} = 1;$

or, *a fraction multiplied by its reciprocal is unity.*

(x.) Division of fractions.

$$\dfrac{N}{D} \div \dfrac{n}{d} = \dfrac{N}{D} \div \dfrac{n}{d} \times \dfrac{n}{d} \times \dfrac{d}{n} \text{ by (ix.)}$$

$$= \dfrac{N}{D} \times \dfrac{d}{n}.$$

In other words, *to divide one fraction by another, invert the divisor and multiply.*

(xi.) Addition or subtraction of fractions. If the denominators are alike, we can proceed as in simple addition and subtraction.

Thus $\dfrac{a}{x} + \dfrac{b}{x} = \dfrac{a+b}{x}.$

(xii.) If the denominators are different we may, by the principle (v.), replace the fractions by equivalent fractions of a common denomination. The product of the denominators will be a suitable common denominator. Thus :—

$$\frac{a}{x} + \frac{b}{y} + \frac{c}{z} = \frac{ayz}{xyz} + \frac{bxz}{xyz} + \frac{cxy}{xyz}$$

$$= \frac{ayz + bxz + cxy}{xyz}.$$

But if any of the denominators have any common factors, a less common denominator can always be found (the L. C. M. of the denominators). Thus :—

$$\frac{a}{yz} + \frac{b}{xz} + \frac{c}{xy} = \frac{ax}{xyz} + \frac{by}{xyz} + \frac{cz}{xyz}$$

$$= \frac{ax + by + cz}{xyz}.$$

EASY EXERCISES IN FRACTIONS.

128. Simplify the following fractions :—

$$\frac{ax}{bx}, \quad \frac{x^2}{2xy}, \quad \frac{x^2}{ax + bx}, \quad \frac{a^3}{a^2x}, \quad \frac{3a^3b^2c}{2ab^2c^3},$$

129. Express the following as simply as possible :—

$$\frac{a}{x} + \frac{x}{y}, \quad \frac{a}{b} + \frac{b}{c} + \frac{c}{a}, \quad 1 \div \left(1 - \frac{1}{a}\right),$$

$$\frac{a-b}{b} + \frac{a+b}{a}, \quad \left(\frac{1}{y} - \frac{1}{x}\right) \div (x - y),$$

$$\frac{b-c}{bc} + \frac{c-a}{ca} + \frac{a-b}{ab}, \quad \frac{1}{x} + \frac{1}{y} + \frac{1}{z}.$$

130. Find the value of each of the following expressions :—

$$\frac{3}{4 \times 5} + \frac{4}{5 \times 3} - \frac{5}{3 \times 4}.$$

$$\frac{7}{24 \times 25} + \frac{24}{7 \times 25} - \frac{25}{7 \times 24}.$$

$$\frac{3}{1 + \dfrac{2}{3 + \frac{4}{5}}}, \qquad \frac{7}{3 - \dfrac{4}{5 - \frac{7}{8}}}, \qquad \frac{8}{4 - \dfrac{5}{5 + \frac{1}{7}}}.$$

$$\tfrac{2}{3}[1 - \tfrac{5}{4}\{1 - \tfrac{4}{7}(1 + \tfrac{3}{4})\}].$$

$$\tfrac{3}{5}[3 - \tfrac{3}{4}\{\tfrac{2}{3} - \tfrac{5}{3}(1 + \tfrac{2}{5}) - \tfrac{1}{2}(3 - \tfrac{1}{3})\}].$$

$$1 - [3 - \tfrac{2}{3}\{1 - \tfrac{3}{4}(1 - \tfrac{7}{8}) + \tfrac{3}{5}(1 + \tfrac{2}{3})\}].$$

131. Simplify :—

$$\frac{a}{x} + \frac{ab}{x^2} + \frac{ab^2}{x^3} + \frac{ab^3}{x^4}.$$

$$\frac{p+q}{p} + \frac{p^2 - q^2}{pq} - \frac{p+q}{q}.$$

$$\frac{y-z}{x} + \frac{z-x}{y} + \frac{x^2 - y^2}{xy}.$$

$$\frac{z^2 - y^2}{yz} - \frac{z+x}{y} - \frac{x-y}{z}.$$

$$\frac{3a + 2b}{a^2} + \frac{5a - 3b}{2ab} - \frac{2a + 7b}{b^2}.$$

$$\frac{a+b}{2a} - \frac{a^2 + b^2}{a^2} + \frac{a^3 + b^3}{2a^3}.$$

132. Find the value of

$$\left(\frac{a}{b} + \frac{b}{a}\right) \div \left(\frac{c}{d} + \frac{d}{c}\right)$$

when $a = 7$, $b = 4$, $c = 8$, $d = 1$.

Also when $a = 7$, $b = 6$, $c = 9$, $d = 2$.

Also when $a = 7$, $b = 2\frac{1}{2}$, $c = 5\frac{1}{2}$, $d = 5$.

133. If $2x = 3y$, find the value of

$$\frac{(3x - y)^2 + (2x - 5y)^2}{(6x - 5y)^2 + (x - y)^2} ;$$

and of

$$\left(\frac{2y - x}{3x - y} + \frac{3x}{4y}\right) \div \frac{x + y}{2x + y}.$$

134. Simplify the following fractions :—

$$\frac{a - \dfrac{ab}{a + b}}{a + \dfrac{ab}{a - b}} \qquad \frac{\dfrac{a + x}{a - x} + \dfrac{a - x}{a + x}}{\dfrac{a + x}{a - x} - \dfrac{a - x}{a + x}} \qquad \frac{x + 2 + \dfrac{1}{x}}{x - \dfrac{1}{x}}$$

$$\frac{1 - \dfrac{1}{x + \dfrac{b}{a}}}{1 + \dfrac{1}{x - \dfrac{b}{a}}} \qquad \frac{\dfrac{2m + n}{m} - \dfrac{2n + m}{n}}{\dfrac{3m + n}{m} + \dfrac{m - n}{n}} \qquad \frac{a}{b + \dfrac{c}{d + \dfrac{e}{f + \dfrac{g}{h}}}}$$

$$\frac{(56x + 3y)^2 + (33x + 41y)^2}{(16x - 27y)^2 + (63x + 31y)^2}$$

$$\frac{1}{1 - \dfrac{1}{1 - \dfrac{1}{1 - x}}} \qquad \frac{20\dfrac{x^2 + y^2}{3x + y} + 3xy\dfrac{3x - y}{x^2 - y^2}}{\dfrac{5x + y}{18} - \dfrac{xy}{x + 4y}}$$

135. Solve the equations :—

$$\frac{3}{x} - \frac{2}{x + 1} = \frac{5}{4(x + 1)}.$$

$$\frac{17}{6x + 17} - \frac{10}{3x - 10} = \frac{1}{1 - 2x}.$$

$$\frac{24}{(x-1)(2x+1)} + \frac{5}{x(2x+1)} = \frac{13}{x(x-1)}.$$

$$\frac{x-b}{a-b} + \frac{x-c}{a-c} = \frac{2x}{a}.$$

$$\frac{ax-b^2}{a-b} - \frac{ax-c^2}{a-c} = \frac{bx-cx}{a}.$$

$$\left(\frac{x}{a} + \frac{x}{b} - 1\right)\left(\frac{x}{a} - \frac{x}{b} + 1\right) + \left(\frac{x}{b} + \frac{x}{c} - 1\right)\left(\frac{x}{b} - \frac{x}{c} + 1\right)$$

$$+ \left(\frac{x}{c} + \frac{x}{a} - 1\right)\left(\frac{x}{c} - \frac{x}{a} + 1\right) = 1.$$

136. Simplify :—

$$\frac{m}{n} - \frac{m-1}{n-1} \qquad \frac{h+k}{h-k} - \frac{h-k}{h+k}$$

$$1 + \frac{2}{x-1} + \frac{1}{(x-1)^2} \qquad 1 - 2\left(\frac{p+1}{q+1}\right) + \left(\frac{p+1}{q+1}\right)^2.$$

137. Simplify :—

$$\frac{1}{a-2b} - \frac{4}{a-b} + \frac{6}{a} - \frac{4}{a+b} + \frac{1}{a+2b}$$

and

$$\frac{1}{x-3y} - \frac{3}{x-y} + \frac{3}{x+y} - \frac{1}{x+3y}.$$

MISCELLANEOUS EXERCISES.

THE following exercises do not involve any new principles, but they are mostly a little more complicated than those which have preceded.

138. If $a = 1$, $b = 2$, $c = 3$, $d = 4$, $e = 5$, show that

$$a^3 + b^3 + c^3 = (a + b + c)^2$$
$$a^3 + b^3 + c^3 + d^3 = (a + b + c + d)^2$$
$$a^3 + b^3 + c^3 + d^3 + e^3 = (a + b + c + d + e)^2.$$

139. Multiply :—

$$(m^2 - n^2)x^2 + (m^2 + n^2)x - 2mn$$
$$\text{by } 2mnx^2 + (m^2 + n^2)x - (m^2 - n^2)$$
$$\text{and } (a + b)^3 + (a - b)^3 \text{ by } (a + b)^3 - (a - b)^3.$$

140. Divide :—

$$(x + y)^5 - x^5 - y^5 \text{ by } x^2 + xy + y^2$$
$$\text{and } (x + h)^3 - 7(x + h)(x + k)^2 + 6(x + k)^3 \text{ by } h - k.$$

141. Divide :—

$$2(x^4 + 1)(y^3 - y) + (x^3 - x)(y^2 + 1)(y^2 + 2y - 1)$$
$$\text{by } 2x^2y + xy^2 - y^2 + x + 1$$
$$\text{and } (a^4 - b^4)(x^4 - y^4) + 4abxy(a^2x^2 - b^2y^2) .$$
$$\text{by } a^2x^2 - b^2y^2 + (bx + ay)^2.$$

142. Divide :—

$$\frac{7}{20} + \frac{16}{15} - \frac{5}{12} \text{ by } \frac{1}{20} + \frac{2}{15} - \frac{1}{12},$$

$$\text{and } \frac{a + 2c}{bc} + \frac{b + 2a}{ca} + \frac{c + 2b}{ab} \text{ by } \frac{1}{bc} + \frac{1}{ca} + \frac{1}{ab},$$

$$\text{and } \frac{b - x}{bc} + \frac{c - x}{ca} + \frac{a - x}{ab} \text{ by } \frac{x - c}{bc} + \frac{x - a}{ca} + \frac{x - b}{ab}.$$

143. Simplify :—

$$x^3 + \cfrac{x^2}{x^2 + \cfrac{1}{x^3 - \cfrac{x^8 + x^3 - 1}{x^5}}}$$

and

$$\cfrac{\dfrac{1}{a} - \dfrac{2}{a+x} + \dfrac{1}{a+2x}}{\dfrac{1}{a} - \dfrac{3}{a+x} + \dfrac{3}{a+2x} - \dfrac{1}{a+3x}}$$

144. Find the value of

$$\frac{(13x + 25)^2 - (12x + 7)^2 - (5x + 24)^2}{(3x - 8)^2 + (4x - 15)^2 - (5x - 17)^2}$$

and of

$$(x + 1)^3 - 2(x + 5)^3 - (x + 9)^3 + 2(x + 11)^3 + (x + 12)^3 - (x + 16)^3$$

145. Show that

$$1 - (a^2 + b^2 + c^2) + bc(1 - b + c) + ca(1 - c + a) + ab(1 - a + b)$$
$$= (1 + b - c)(1 + c - a)(1 + a - b)$$

146. If $x = a + d$, $y = b + d$, $z = c + d$, prove that
$x^2 + y^2 + z^2 - yz - zx - xy = a^2 + b^2 + c^2 - bc - ca - ab$.

147. If $y + z = a$, $z + x = b$, $x + y = c$, prove that
$x^2 + y^2 + z^2 - yz - zx - xy = a^2 + b^2 + c^2 - bc - ca - ab$.

148. Show that

$$pqr\left(1 - \frac{x}{p} - \frac{y}{q} - \frac{z}{r}\right) - xyz\left(1 - \frac{p}{x} - \frac{q}{y} - \frac{r}{z}\right)$$
$$= (p - x)(q - y)(r - z)$$

D

and that

$$(ax + b)(bx + c)(cx + a) - (ax + c)(cx + b)(bx + a)$$
$$= x(1 - x)(b - c)(c - a)(a - b).$$

149. Solve the equations:—

$$(10x - 11)(11 + 2x) + (5x - 11)(11 + 3x)$$
$$+ (7x - 11)(11 - 5x) = 0.$$
$$(x + 2m + 2m^2)^2 = (x + 2m)^2 + (2m + 2m^2)^2$$
$$(x - 2n + 1)^2 = (x - 2n)^2 + (2n - 1)^2.$$

150. Solve the equations :—

$$(a^2x - 2ac + 1)(b^2x + 2bc + 1) = (abx + ac - bc - 1)^2.$$
$$(ax + bx - a)(ax - bx + b) + (bx + cx - b)(bx - cx + c)$$
$$+ (cx + ax - c)(cx - ax + a) = 0.$$

151. Show that if $\quad p + q + r = 0$,

$$p^4 + q^4 + r^4 = \tfrac{1}{2}(p^2 + q^2 + r^2)^2.$$

152. Show that if x, y, z are any three consecutive integers

$$(x + y + z)^3 - 3(x^3 + y^3 + z^3) = 18xyz.$$

153. One bought four horses for £180. The second cost £4 more than the first, the third cost twice as much as the second, and the fourth three times as much as the first ; what did each cost?

154. A payment of £19, 11s. 6d. was made in gold, silver, and copper. The silver was 11d. more than $\frac{1}{6}$th of the gold, and the copper was 6d. more than $\frac{1}{11}$th of the silver ; how much was there of each ?

155. Show how to divide 29 shillings among 3 men, 5 women, and 4 children, so that each woman may get $\frac{5}{7}$ths of a man's share, and each child $\frac{1}{4}$th of a man's share and woman's share together.

156. A man lays out half his money in black tea at 3s. per lb., and the other half in green tea at 5s. per lb. At what price per lb. must he sell the mixture so as to make a profit equal to $\frac{1}{5}$th of his outlay ?

157. A boy does half as much work as a man, and gets one-third of a man's wages. How much shall we have to pay 5 men and 4 boys to reap a field, if it cost £7 when men only are employed ?

158. If $a = 1$, $b = 2$, $c = 3$, $d = 4$, $e = 5$, $f = 6$, show that

$$a^4 + b^4 = bc(b + c) \left(\frac{bc}{10} - \frac{1}{30} \right)$$

$$a^4 + b^4 + c^4 = cd(c + d) \left(\frac{cd}{10} - \frac{1}{30} \right)$$

$$a^4 + b^4 + c^4 + d^4 = de(d + e) \left(\frac{de}{10} - \frac{1}{30} \right)$$

$$a^4 + b^4 + c^4 + d^4 + e^4 = ef(e + f) \left(\frac{ef}{10} - \frac{1}{30} \right).$$

159. Divide $a^4(b - c) + b^4(c - a) + c^4(a - b)$
     by $a^2(b - c) + b^2(c - a) + c^2(a - b)$.

160. Simplify :—

$$\frac{x + 8}{(x - 15)(x - 17)} + \frac{x + 15}{(x - 8)(x - 17)} - \frac{x + 17}{(x - 8)(x - 15)}.$$

161. Solve the equations :—
$$(b - c)(x - a)^3 + (c - a)(x - b)^3 + (a - b)(x - c)^3 = 0.$$
$$(m - n)(x - a)^2 + (n - l)(x - b)^2 + (l - n)(x - c)^2 = 0.$$

162. At 3 o'clock the minute-hand of a watch is 15 minute-divisions behind the hour-hand. The minute-hand takes one minute, and the hour-hand twelve

minutes, to traverse a minute division.   In how many
minutes will the minute-hand overtake the hour-hand?

163. At what time between 9 and 10 o'clock are
the two hands together ?

164. If $a = 1$, $b = 2$, $c = 3$, $d = 4$, $e = 5$, $f = 6$, $g = 7$,
show that

$$a^2 + b^2 + c^2 = \frac{cd(c+d)}{6}$$

$$a^2 + b^2 + c^2 + d^2 = \frac{de(d+e)}{6}$$

$$a^2 + b^2 + c^2 + d^2 + e^2 = \frac{ef(e+f)}{6}$$

$$a^2 + b^2 + c^2 + d^2 + e^2 + f^2 = \frac{fg(f+g)}{6}.$$

165. Divide

$$\frac{1}{1-5y} - \frac{5}{1-3y} + \frac{10}{1-y} - \frac{10}{1+y} + \frac{5}{1+3y} - \frac{1}{1+5y}$$

by the product of

$$\frac{1}{1-5y} - \frac{2}{1-3y} + \frac{1}{1-y} \text{ and } \frac{1}{1+y} - \frac{2}{1+3y} + \frac{1}{1+5y}.$$

166. Solve the equations :—

$$\left. \begin{array}{l} x + y = 2a \\ x - y = 2b \end{array} \right\}$$

$$\left. \begin{array}{l} (m+n)x - (m-n)y = 4mn \\ (m-n)x + (m+n)y = 2m^2 - 2n^2 \end{array} \right\}$$

$$\left. \begin{array}{l} -x + y + z = 2a \\ x - y + z = 2b \\ x + y - z = 2c \end{array} \right\}$$

167. Find x and y from the equations

$$ax + by = ay - bx = a^2 + b^2.$$

168. Find x and y from the equations

$$y - x = a - b = \frac{ax - by}{c}.$$

169. In a racecourse of 240 yards, A can give B 48 yards' start, and B can give C 30 yards' start; how many yards can A give C.

170. After walking at the rate of $3\frac{1}{2}$ miles per hour until the number of miles left of my journey was the same as the number of hours I had been walking, I quickened my pace to 4 miles per hour, and accomplished the whole distance in 2 hours 55 minutes. What was the length of my journey?

171. If $a + h = b$, $a + 2h = c$, $a + 3h = d$, $a + 4h = e$, $a + 5h = f$, prove that

$$a + b + c + d + e + f = 3(a + f) ;$$

and $def - abc = 3h(bc + cd + de)$;

and $\dfrac{1}{ab} + \dfrac{1}{bc} + \dfrac{1}{cd} + \dfrac{1}{de} + \dfrac{1}{ef} = \dfrac{h}{f} - \dfrac{h}{a}$;

and $\dfrac{1}{abc} + \dfrac{1}{bcd} + \dfrac{1}{cde} + \dfrac{1}{def} = \dfrac{2h}{ef} - \dfrac{2h}{ab}$.

172. Find x, y, z, from the equations

$$\left. \begin{array}{c} y + z - bc = z + x - ca = x + y - ab \\[2mm] \dfrac{x}{a} + \dfrac{y}{b} + \dfrac{z}{c} = 2\,(a + b + c). \end{array} \right\}$$

173. Having 75 minutes at my disposal, how far can I go in a coach at $6\frac{2}{3}$ miles an hour, having to walk back at $3\frac{3}{4}$ miles per hour?

174. A publisher found that setting up the type of a book cost half as much as he had paid to the author for copyright, and that after the type was set up the further cost of producing the book was 3d. per copy. He then calculated that if he sold 4000 copies at the proposed price, his profit would be twice the cost of copyright ; but if he sold 12,000 copies at half the price, his profit would be three times the cost of copyright. Find the price at which the book was to be sold.

175. 3 boats started at the same moment, at intervals of 100 yards apart ; in 6 minutes the third overtook the second, and in 2 minutes more it overtook the first. How soon will the second overtake the first ?

176. The geese in a poultry-yard are worth as much as the turkeys and ducks together, and the number of geese is the same as the number of pence a goose is worth. The number of turkeys is also equal to the number of pence a turkey is worth, and the number of ducks equal to the number of pence a duck is worth. The number of geese is 10 less than $\frac{5}{4}$ths of the number of turkeys, and the number of ducks 22 less than $\frac{3}{4}$ths of the number of turkeys. How many were there of each?

ANSWERS.

1.	4	−2	−4	100	−98
	−9	−11	13	0	−6
	1	−1	2	3	−3.

2.	5	−1	−3	101	−97
	−8	−10	14	1	−5
	2	0	3	4	−2.

3.	6	0	−2	102	−96
	−7	−9	15	2	−4
	3	1	4	5	−1.

4.	8	2	0	104	−94
	−5	−7	17	4	−2
	5	3	6	7	1.

5.	−21	−19	−10	9	11	20.

6.	−10000	−100	0	10	1000.

7.	−1000	−10	0	100	10000.

8.	0	0	0	0	0	0.

9.	8	10	5	6
	2	10	10
	4	5	24
	4	13	40
	5	11	16.

10. 2d.,   − 2d.,   − 6d.,   − 5d.,   0,   3d.,   − 10d.,   − 1d.,

11. − 8d.,   0,   − 11d.,   − 11d.,   2d.,   − 2d.,
11d.,   − 2d.,   − 8d.,   0,   − 15d.

12. − 19d.

13. Ada, 9d. ; Mary, 1d. ; Jane, 5d. ; Fanny, 11d.

14. 10   − 3   3   0   5   9
4   − 4   − 4   12   − 12   − 30.

15. 2   8   − 2   − 8   2   − 2
− 2   22   0   20   2   22
0   24   − 22   2   − 20   0
− 22   − 2   − 24   0   − 10   12
33   − 28   2   3   − 42   32.

16. £40.   **17.** He takes − 30 pounds.   £30 richer.

18. £30.

19.   − 1   1   − 6   0   6
1575   113   − 100   1000   − 1000
− 1102   − 510   − 499   − 501   − 1000.

20. 7   5   22   2   3
− 8   0   5   − 17   3.

21. − 12,   − 5,   − 25,   − 28,   − 12.

22.   − 60   − 96   − 16
− 60   − 60   − 3
60   − 300   − 3
60   − 16   1.

23.   − 60   60
− 60   60
− 1   1
1.

24. 2160   − 1620   − 1296   1080   − 810   − 540
− 648   405   360   324   − 240   − 216
− 1   − 1.

25. 1,　　152,　　-6,　　-42.

26.　　45　　　　12　　　　6
　　　　-5　　　-45　　　4
　　　　-3　　　　0　　　　0.

27. -6,　　　0,　　　42,　　　21,　　　42,　　　7,　　　8.

28.　8,　　　16,　　　19.

29. 43,　　　71,　　　13,　　　-19,　　　26.

31. $13p + 5f + 7a$.

32. $5p + 7f + 7a$　　　　$12p + 5f + 7a$.

34. $2f - 2a$　　　$- 3p - 1f + 5a$
　　　$4a - 4p$　　　$4p - 1f - 1a$.

35. $- 3p + 6a$.

36.　　　$12f$　　　　　　$12p - 5f$　　　$3p + 10a$
　　$11a + 17f + 6p$　　　$8p - 1a - 6f$　　　$3f$.

37. $6p - 16a - 6f$　　　$2p + 4a + 3f$　　　$9p + 6a + 9f$
　　　　$4p + 4a$　　　$1f$　　　$1p + 5a + 1f$.

38.　　　2　　　　　82
　　　-10　　　　-128.

39. $1s + 6d + 11h$,　　　　　0.

40. $2s + 2h + 6d$　　　$4s + 2h - 8d$
　　　$4s - 10h$　　　$4s - h - 5d$.

41.　　1242　　　　　0
　　　412　　　　384
　　　-720　　　-280.

42. $19a + 2b + 2c$　　　$a + b + c$　　　$2a + 2b + 2c$.

43. $9x - 6y + 4z$　　　$p + q + r$.

44. $a + 2b - 6c$ $2x - 4y - 4z$

        $2z$ $2y - 2z$

   $2b + 2c - 2d$ $b + c$

   $3x - y + 2z$ $a - c$ $a - 2b + c$ $2a - b - c$

   $2x + y + z$ $2p + 8q - 2r.$

45. $7a - 2b - c$ $22a - 3b - 14c$ $x + 13y + 4z$

   $3 - 4x$ $48x - 301$ $22x + 8$ $26a - 10b - 25c.$

46. $4aa - 12ab + 9bb$ $3xxx + 5xx - 3x + 5.$

47. 0 $2ay$ $ac - bc$ $xx + yy + zz$ 0

     $aa + bb + cc - 2ab + 2ac - 2bc$

      $aaa - bbb$ $- xxz - yyz.$

48. $- 2ab - 5ac + 2bc$ x $3xxx - 5yyy + 2zzz$

     $10ac - 29ad + 12bc - 3cd$

   $xxxx - axxx + bbxx - cccx + dddd.$

49. $2ax + 2by$ $2aa + 2ab$ $xxx + 9x.$

51. $xx + ax + bx + ab$ $3xxx - 7xx + 9x + 10$

       $3xxx + 13xx - 50$ $xxxx - 16.$

    $xxx - yyy$ $xxxx + xxyy + yyyy.$

52. $8aaa + 6abc - bbb + ccc$

    $15aaaa + 46aa - a - 60$

    $16aaaa + 4aa + 25.$

53. $4xx + 12x + 9$

   $xxxx - 4xxxy + 12xxyy - 16xyyy + 16yyyy$

   $xxx + yyy + zzz - 3xyz.$

54. xx $xx - 1$ x $16x$ $xx + 4x$ $xx.$

55. $aaaa + bbbb + cccc - 2aabb - 2aacc - 2bbcc$

   $xxxxxxxx - yyyyyyyy.$

57.

x^5	$6x^5$	$20x^6$
x^7	$2x^6$	$16x^8$
$9a^6$	$5a^4$	x^8
$6x^5y^5$	a^5x^4	a^6x^6
$2a^8x^{10}$	$x^2y^3z^4$	$30a^{11}$
	x^3y^3	x^6y^6.

58. $9a^2 \qquad 16a^2b^2 \qquad 8x^3 \qquad 25x^4y^2 \qquad 81x^4$

$a^2 - 2ab + b^2 \quad x^2+2xy+y^2 \quad x^2+6x+9 \quad 4x3-12x+9$

$25a^2+40ab+16b^2 \qquad 4x^2-4x+1 \qquad a^3+3a^2b+3ab^2+b^3$

$x^3-3x^2y+3xy^2-y^3 \quad x^2+3x+3+1 \quad x^4-2x^3+3x^2-2x+1.$

59. $2x^2-3x+9 \qquad x^4-16$

$9x^2-25 \qquad 2x^3-3x^2-10x+15$

$a^3-11a^2+31a-12 \quad x^4+x^2+1 \quad 15a^4+32a^3-8a-15$

$156m^4-125m^3n+5mn^3-156n^4 \qquad x^6-2x^3+1$

$a^6+16a^3+64.$

60. $8x^2+18y^2 \qquad 13x^2+13y^2 \qquad x^3+y^3 \qquad x^3+y^3+z^3-3xyz$

$2ab-2bc+2cd-2da \quad -4ab \quad 18ac \quad 2yz+18xz-4xy.$

61. $25 \qquad 0 \qquad 0 \qquad 0 \qquad 0.$

62.

3	$3x$	$3y$
$2x$	$-6y^2$	$2xy$
a^2b^2c	$-a^2b$	$2r$
abc	a^2c	$-x$

$-4a^3b^2c \quad 3a^2b \quad 2x+3y \quad 2x+3y \quad a^2-2ab+b^2-a+3b.$

64. $x-1 \quad a-2 \quad a^2-2a-2 \quad x-a+y-b \quad ax-bx-ab$

$2x^2-3x+3 \qquad 3x^3+9x^2+7x-1 \qquad 5a^2+13a+12.$

65. $a^2-ax-6x^2 \qquad x^2+y^2 \qquad m^2-n^2 \qquad x^3+x^2y+xy^2+y^3$

$x^4-x^3y+x^2y^2-xy^3+y^4 \qquad a^2+b^2+c^2-ab-ac-bc$

$a^3+3a^2x+3ax^2+x^3 \quad x^4-ax^3+x^3-ax^2+bx^2+x^2-ax+x+1.$

66. 3   −3   55   81.

67. $m+n+2$ $a^4+2a^2b^2+b^4.$

68. 1   1   0   3   1   2   −1   −4   3   1   2   0   0.

69. 0   0   0.   **70.** 0   −1   0.

71. 0   0   0   0   24.

72. 73. 74.   False   True when $x=2$
     True when $x=2$ True when $x=4$
     True when $x=3$ True when $x=4$

75.   True when $x=2$ True when $x=2$ or 5
     True when $x=2$ or 3   True when $x=3$ or 5
     True when $x=3$ True when $x=5$
        True when $x=2$ or 3 or 5.

76. 12   13   −4   −4   0 $5\frac{1}{4}$ $\frac{1}{20}$ $-\frac{1}{5}$ $-\frac{20}{7}$ 1.

78. 8   6   3   4   3   13   7   10.

79. 5   7   2   9   6   7 $2\frac{1}{2}.$

80. 2   3   2   2 $2\frac{1}{2}$ −12 $\frac{1}{10}$ $\frac{4}{5}.$

82. 24   3   4   3   3   12   7   8   3 $\frac{1}{6}$ 11   5   4.

83. $a-b$ a b b $\frac{2}{3}c$ $3a+2b$ $a+b+c$
     $m+n$ $a+b$ $\frac{1}{4}(a+b+c+d).$

85. 8.   **86.** 100.   **87.** 4.   **88.** $3\frac{1}{2}.$ **89.** 13.

90. 3.   **91.** 4, 5, 6.   **92.** 7, 8, 9, 10.

93. 66 boys and 65 girls.   **94.** 105, 35.

95. Each side is 20 feet.   **96.** 20, 14.

97. 29, 17.   **98.** 40, 24, 20.

100. $x=10, y=3$;　　$x=4, y=3$;　　$x=4, y=7$;
　　　$x=5, y=4$;　　$x=5, y=3$;　　$x=7, y=6$;
　　　$x=4, y=5$;　　$x=5, y=2$;　　$x=4, y=-4$;
　　　$x=26, y=5$;　　$x=1, y=1$;　　$x=4, y=5$.

101. $x=3, y=10$;　　$x=7, y=3$;　　$x=9, y=4$;
　　　$x=6, y=7$;　　$x=3, y=2$;　　$x=3, y=3$;
　　　$x=3, y=2$;　　$x=2, y=3$;　　$x=2, y=4$.

103.　$x=1, y=2, z=1$.　　$x=3, y=2, z=5$.
　　　$x=4, y=5, z=7$.　　$x=12, y=13, z=14$.

104. John, £20 ; Tom, £30 ; James, £10.

105. John, 15 years ; Tom, 10 ; James, 9.

106. Jane, 8 shillings ; Ann, 4 ; Mary, 3.

107. 26.　　　**108.** 56, 35.　　　**109.** 18, 14.

110. John, 20 ; Tom, 10 ; Dick, 8.

111. 17, 23.　　**112.** 7, 12.　　**113.** 40 lbs.　　**114.** 54.

115. Man, 5s. ; boy, 3s.　　　　**116.** Man, 5s. ; boy, 1s.

117. Penny, $\frac{1}{3}$ oz. ; halfpenny, $\frac{1}{6}$ oz.

118. 18 fourpenny and 36 threepenny pieces.

119. 6 sixpenny, 6 fourpenny, and 8 threepenny pieces.

120. 3 hours.　　　**121.** 135 pence, 210 halfpence.

122. 20 miles.　　　**123.** John, 7d. ; Tom, 5d.

124. G.C.M. 6, 12, 7, 37, 125, 8, $2a^2b^2$, abc, y^2z, n, r, 12, ab, x, x^3.　　L.C.M., 660, 120, 441, 3330, 5000, 128000, $24a^3b^3$, $a^2b^2c^2$, xy^3z^3, mnr, $lmnr$, $360xyz$, abc, $2a^2$.

127.

G.C.M.	L.C.M.
$x-2$	x^3-5x^2+8x-4
$x-1$	$x^2-8x^2+19x-12$
$p-q$	$p^3-8p^2q+19pq^2-12q^3$
$m+1$	$18m^3+27m^2+10m+1$
$a-b$	$a^4+a^3b-ab^3-b^4$
$a+b$	$a^7-a^6b+a^5b^2+a^2b^5-ab^6+b^7$
a^3+a^2b	$a^2b(a^2-b^2)$
$x^2-4xy+4y^2$	$x^5-2x^4y-8x^3y^2+16x^2y^3+16xy^4-32y^5.$

128. $\quad \dfrac{a}{b} \qquad \dfrac{x}{2y} \qquad \dfrac{x}{a+b} \qquad \dfrac{a}{x} \qquad \dfrac{3a^2}{2c^2}.$

129. $\quad \dfrac{ay+x^2}{xy} \qquad \dfrac{a^2c+b^2a+c^2b}{abc} \qquad \dfrac{a}{a-1} \qquad \dfrac{a^2+b^2}{ab} \qquad \dfrac{1}{xy}$

$$0 \qquad \dfrac{yz+zx+xy}{xyz}.$$

130. $\quad 0 \qquad 0 \qquad \dfrac{57}{29} \qquad \dfrac{231}{67} \qquad \dfrac{288}{109} \qquad \dfrac{2}{3} \qquad \dfrac{63}{20} \qquad -\dfrac{35}{48}.$

131. $\quad \dfrac{ax^3+abx^2+ab^2x+ab^3}{x^4} \qquad 0 \qquad \dfrac{xz-yz}{xy} \qquad -\dfrac{xy+xz}{yz}$

$$\dfrac{4b^3+3ab^2-9a^2b-4a^3}{2a^2b^2} \qquad \dfrac{b(a^2-2ab+b^2)}{2a^3}.$$

132. $\quad \dfrac{2}{7} \qquad \dfrac{3}{7} \qquad \dfrac{11}{7}.$ **133.** $1 \qquad \dfrac{21}{35}.$

134. $\quad \dfrac{a-b}{a+b} \qquad \dfrac{a^2+x^2}{2ax} \qquad \dfrac{x+1}{x-1} \qquad \dfrac{a^2x^2-a^2x+ab-b^2}{a^2x^2+a^2x+ab-b^2}$

$$\dfrac{n-m}{n+m} \qquad \dfrac{adfh+adg+aeh}{bdfh+bdg+beh+cfh+cg} \qquad 1 \qquad x$$

$$\dfrac{18(x+4y)(4x^2+3xy-5y^2)}{(3x+y)(x^2-y^2)}.$$

135. $\quad 12 \qquad \dfrac{1}{4} \qquad 6 \qquad a \qquad a \qquad \dfrac{2abc}{bc+ca+ab}.$

136. $\dfrac{n-m}{n^2-n}$ $\dfrac{4hk}{h^2-k^2}$ $\dfrac{x^2}{(x-1)^2}$ $\left(\dfrac{p-q}{q-1}\right)^2$.

137. $\dfrac{24b^2}{a(a^2-b^2)(a^2-4b^2)}$ $\dfrac{48y^3}{(x^2-y^2)(x^2-9y^2)}$.

139. $2mn(m^2-n^2)(x^4+1)+(m^2+n^2)(m^2+2mn-n^2)(x^3-x)$.
$4ab(3a^4+10a^2b^2+3b^4)$.

140. $5xy(x+y)$ $h^2+hk-6k^2+3xh-11xk-4x^2$.

141. $x^2(y^2-1)+x(y^2+1)-2y$, $a^2x^2-b^2y^2-(bx-ay)^2$.

142. 10, $a+b+c$,   1.

143. 1. $1+\dfrac{a}{3x}$.

144. 141. -184.

149. $\frac{1}{2}$, 1, $2n^2$.

150. c^2. $\frac{1}{2}$.

153. £24, £28, £56, £72.

154. Gold, £16, 10s. ; silver, £2, 15s. 11d. ; copper, 5s. 7d.

155. Man, 3s. 6d. ; woman, 2s. 6d. ; child, 1s. 6d.

156. 4s. 6d.

157. £6, 6s. 8d.

159. $a^2+b^2+c^2+bc+ca+ab$.

160. $\dfrac{x^2}{(x-8)(x-15)(x-17)}$.

161. $\dfrac{a+b+c}{3}$ $\dfrac{a^2(m-n)+b^2(n-l)+c^2(l-m)}{2a(m-n)+2b(n-l)+2c(l-m)}$.

162. $16\frac{4}{11}$.   **163.** $10\frac{10}{11}$ minutes before 10.

165. $60y$.

166. $x=a+b, \quad y=a-b.$ $\qquad x=m+n, \; y=m-n.$
$x=b+c, \; y=c+a, \; z=a+b.$

167. $x=a-b.$ $\qquad\qquad y=a+b.$

168. $x=b+c.$ $\qquad\qquad y=a+c.$

169. 72. $\qquad\qquad$ **170.** $10\frac{1}{2}.$

172. $x=a(b+c).$ $\qquad y=b(c+a).$ $\qquad z=c(a+b).$

173. 3 miles. $\qquad\qquad$ **174.** 2 shillings.

175. In 4 minutes more.

176. 50 geese, 48 turkeys, 14 ducks.

PRINTED BY PHILIP AND SON, LIVERPOOL.